Deadly Restoration

A Douglas Lake Mystery

Eric M. Howe

Dear Reader -

This is my third novel in the fiction genre. My first two were based upon the history of science, involving a contemporary search to recreate Isaac Newton's lost alchemical formula for the secret of consciousness.

Deadly Restoration is my first mystery, and I look forward to writing the sequel in early 2019.

I hope you enjoy the story. If so, please recommend it. It is available on Amazon in both hard copy and Kindle versions – though I am certainly happy to send an electronic version free to anyone who wishes. Mind you, this isn't my "day job" but rather a hobby.

If you have feedback … please reach out. I take constructive criticism well ☺.

Kindly,
Eric   emhowe@assumption.edu

Books:
- A Paxton Year
- Cycle of the Seasons
- Illumination: The Newton Secret
- Entanglement: The Newton Secret, Book 2
- Deadly Restoration: A Douglas Lake Mystery
- Douglas Lake Essays

Copyright © 2019 Eric M. Howe
All rights reserved.
ISBN-13: 9781729469538

FORWARD

Though this is a work of fiction, it is based loosely on real issues concerning the restoration of the Maple River in Northern Michigan. Of course, the characters in this book are imaginary and should in no way be associated with any of the actual parties regarding the project or the surrounding area.

I share the main character's deep feelings for the lake and its people, having been so fortunate that my parents gave me the childhood to cultivate a connection I can't adequately convey in words alone.

Through the years, as one generation slowly gives way to the next, the lake remains a patient fixture, sharing its profound beauty for those who return summer after summer.

On the berm where the big pine emerges from the sandy soil, old needles and cast-offs of unused cones litter the ground. Mixed within are sparse tendrils of blueberry vines, with small green leaves that splay delicately against the carpet of sand and needled earth. Stonecrop thrives here amid dappled sunlight from the branches overhead. Its tiny succulent leaves somehow hold enough moisture for the faded yellow blossoms to form in early July.

    This pattern repeats itself along the neglected shores, where sunlight and wind and sandy soil give home to rising pines. It is where needles carpet the warm ground, shaped into nature's patterns by strong winds that come across the lake.

Image of Douglas Lake

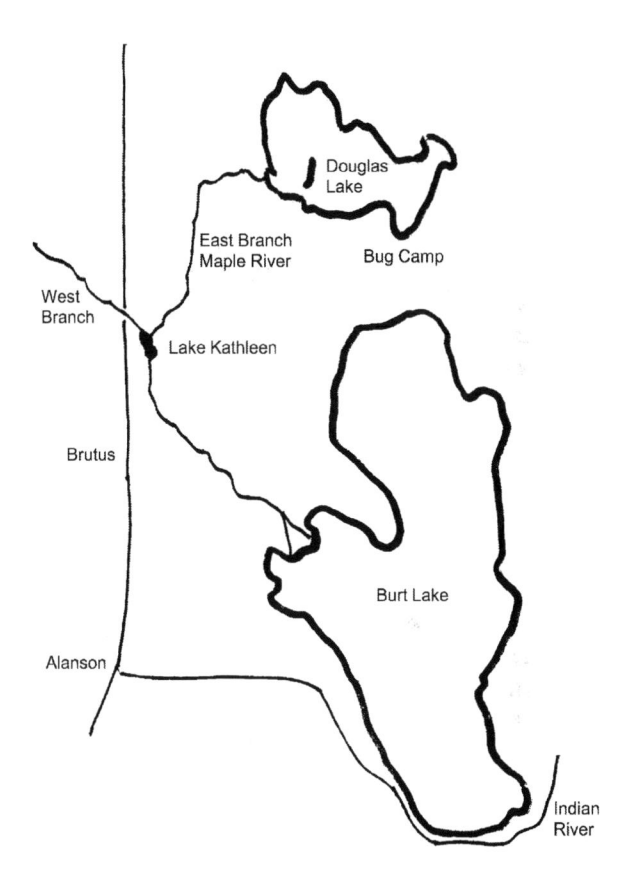

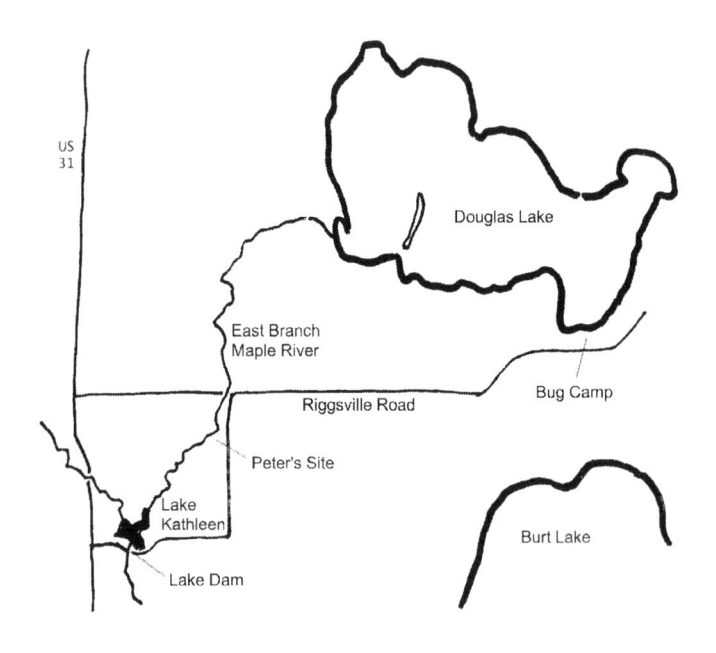

Prologue

A patch of sunlight penetrated through the canopy, highlighting several sedges against the contrast of bleached sandbar from which they emerged. A pair of Ebony Jewelwings fluttered haphazardly, their inky black bodies like moving shadows against the deep greens of the background shore.

The sand formed at a place where the river curved back upon itself, entering the dim light of the thicker boreal forest downstream a dozen yards away from where the woman stood knee deep in waders beneath the shade of an overhanging white cedar. She bent over and thrust a hand that held a metal rod into the cold water, placing it an inch above the river bottom as she turned her attention to a meter gripped in her other. The water moved quickly near the shore as it cut into the sharp bank around the outer curve, flowing underneath the skeletal remains of several deadfalls and slowing where the river straightened slightly into a deeper pool.

She took another reading, barely feeling the stony bottom against her hand as she moved the probe several feet upstream where the flow quickened. She paused, sensing something out of ordinary from the normal background noises of lapping water and the forest birdsong.

"Hello?" she said curiously, jerking her head upright in the same way a deer reacts unexpectedly to something in the forest. A cracking twig gave way to the movement of a group of emerald ferns along the bank. She raised her hand with the monitor to shield her eyes. "Who's there?" she said, watching as a backlit figure stepped gingerly off the bank into the shallow water and approached slowly with an extended finger held upward across his lips, signaling for her to remain quiet.

"What in the world-" she began.

He repeated the gesture insistently to silence her and pointed with the same finger cautiously to the woods over her shoulder.

She slowly turned her head and allowed her gaze to sweep the dark woods behind her, whispering as she heard his footfalls break the water. "What is it you want me to −" cut off by the searing impact to the back of her head, aware in an instant of blinding pain as she fell forward into the cold river, her eyes slowly closing as darkness enveloped her senses.

Chapter 1

A pair of worn bells sounded as the door swung inward, causing a heavyset woman to glance upward as she poured coffee.

"Well, it's about that time," she said loudly enough the majority of customers stopped what they were doing and fixed on Rick as he entered. She finished filling the cup and turned to face him squarely across the restaurant. "The black flies and mosquitoes have returned, so I knew it wouldn't be long before *your types* arrived." She chuckled slightly and nodded her head curtly to an empty table near the far wall. "Have a seat, teach. I'll be over shortly with a fresh pot, and you can tell me how glad you are to see me."

Rick smiled as he moved to the empty table, skirting around the chair of a man who had evidently finished eating too much food and now sat nearly prostrate from his plate, partially blocking the small path between. "Excuse me, sir," he said, nodding sympathetically to the man's wife, who sat opposite and bore an expression of embarrassment.

"For the love of God, pull in your chair, Harry," she blurted, seeing Rick struggle sideways to navigate the space between the back of her husband's head and the person sitting comfortably at the nearest table.

This startled the man from what must have been digestive reverie, for his legs jerked slightly, causing his chair to push backward and catching Rick's foot. He lurched forward and reflexively reached for a large wooden support beam nearby, saving himself from a complete face plant on the worn floor.

"Things were quiet till you arrived," offered Jan sarcastically as she approached, waving her hand gently to silence the man who was about to offer his apologies. "No need, Harry. Isn't that right *Erasmus*?"

Rick winced at her emphasis. "No harm." He lowered himself into the rustic chair and positioned it near the table. "I know how good it feels to finish one of the Deli's big breakfasts." He winked kindly to the man's wife. "Sometimes they nearly have to cart me out of here I'm so stuffed."

"Sometimes we want to bounce you out, is what you mean," Jan replied, quickly scanning the room to make sure the other tables were happily served. She took the seat opposite his and poured them both a cup of coffee. "And don't give me that hurt look."

"I just got here, and you're starting in like we've already been through the summer season."

"Exactly." She eyed him narrowly. "*Your* bunch tends to loiter a little too long for good business."

"But we do provide business!" he said teasingly.

Jan huffed and raised her cup. "Here's to rough starts, I guess."

"That wasn't my -" He stopped and took a deep breath. "Oh the hell with it." He lifted his cup in return. "Here's to another summer." Rick took a slow sip and allowed his eyes to wander about the room. "I see not much has changed."

The Brutus Camp Deli was a single room log cabin, with pine siding from floor to open ceiling and rustic wooden furniture throughout. The interior decoration consisted largely of hunting and fishing trophies and accouterments, covering nearly every square inch of available wall space and creating a decidedly unique northern woods flavor. There were approximately a dozen tables of various sizes, with nearly half occupied by a mixture of customers, from locals to tourists. The latter were easy to distinguish with their shorts and t-shirts, while the regular patrons tended to favor flannel and jeans, even in the heart of summer. Then there were the transients, like the faculty and students from the biological station, who spent the summer in classes and research on the campus several miles away at Douglas Lake, making frequent forays to the Deli for what was arguably the best cooked breakfasts and lunches for miles. Given the paucity of restaurants up north, this distinction wasn't all that impressive.

Jan followed his gaze and resettled on his bemused expression. "Hell no. Nothing's changed here in twenty years, nor is it likely to for the next twenty."

"Like you?"

"Watch it," she said evenly. "I've changed a little, as I'm sure you can tell. Yes, there's a little more of me to love, which I'll thank you not to comment. Isn't it early in the summer to start throwing barbs?"

"You started it," he beamed.

She laughed, warmly this time. "Things do get a little stale here in the winter. The hunting and snow mobile crowds are too predictable, and it seems to last longer and longer." She paused and took a sip. "Truth is I'm glad for the change in clientele."

"You mean you actually look forward to us summer people?"

She smiled, noting his expression of false belief. "Look *Erasmus*," she said, emphasizing his Christian name again. "Perhaps you've caught me in a rare moment of weakness, but I have been looking forward to all of you arriving north for the summer. It peels back the years." Rick watched as she idly rotated a narrow watchband about her pudgy wrist and then met his gaze vulnerably. "Does that seem silly?"

He smiled. "Nope. Not at all, Jan. I feel the same way when I get here, especially when the students arrive and the camp session gets underway. Reminds me of those summers long ago when we were all running around together." He suddenly eyed her critically. "And what's with the Erasmus thing?"

She grinned impishly. "I know it bothers you. Always did. Not too many Erasmuses around here up north. Kinda distinguishes you among the flannel crowd."

"I'll let that slide," Rick replied. "And that's only because we go way back."

"Would you rather I shout "Professor"?

Rick chuckled, shaking his head slightly. "God no. That's almost as bad."

"So what do your students call you?"

"Rick is fine, or Dr. Parsons if it has to be formal, which it rarely does. At least, things shouldn't be formal up north."

She spied a customer trying to get her attention and rose slowly. "Back in a jiff. Beverly probably wants the bill." She started then turned her head back. "Do you know Bev?"

He simply shook his head.

"I think she's got a place on the south shore of Douglas. I'll ask her. Be right back."

Rick took a longer sip of coffee and turned his attention to a small pamphlet on the table, wedged within a ring holder between the salt and pepper dispensers. It was an advertisement for the Maple River Outfitters, boasting guided fly fishing excursions on the upper branches of the river. The cover photo displayed the owner standing hip deep in the water next to what must have been a client, the latter proudly holding forth a large rainbow trout between two outstretched hands. Included was text about the superlatives of fishing this stretch of northern Michigan and listed their hours of operation and various rate packages. Rick turned the card over and casually studied the map, depicting the general flow of the East Branch of the Maple, from where it emerged after leaving Douglas Lake until it wound loosely downstream and merged with the West Branch below Pellston at Lake Kathleen.

Jan rejoined him. "Bev's on the south side alright. Didn't know your name either. Said something about the South and North not recognizing one another, which I thought was funny." She jerked a thumb at the advertisement. "You want me to put in a good word to Mike about you?"

Rick failed to understand her meaning. "You know this guy?"

"Mike? Yep, he's the owner – the fella on the front side next to the client." She pursed her lips as if trying to govern how much to reveal. "He's a local."

"Ahh," Rick said simply, knowing the north woods was like a small town in a big domain.

"Aw, the heck with it," she added. "We went to high school together."

He smirked and adjusted his voice, using a snobbish impersonation. "Another product of Harbor Springs?"

"I thought we agreed to be nice?" she replied. "Mike's like me, grew up in the –"

"Rural side?" he offered.

Jan chuckled. "That'll do. Yeah, the rural side of Harbor."

"How come he never hung around with us back when?"

"Because Mike was a jackass then, that's why. And,

he's still a jackass now, twenty years later."

"And you were going to put in a good word for me?"

"I was only kidding." She took the card from his hand and turned it so that they both could read the front face. "Mike came in here about a month ago acting all friendly and asked if I'd be willing to display these cards for a month or so. I figured it was no big deal and said fine, so here they are."

"He takes clients up the Maple?"

"Yep. And from what I hear, he's actually a pretty good fishing guide – knows the river very well, knows how to time the hatches and the weather. He's made a fairly good seasonal business of it."

"The map on the back shows the river all the way into Douglas."

Jan turned the card over and studied the picture. "So?"

Rick pointed to an area well upstream from Lake Kathleen, where the East Branch curved back upon itself. "There's a lot of active research in this area of the Maple from colleagues at the biological station. Does he go upstream that far? It's pretty narrow in that stretch."

Jan shrugged. "You'd have to ask him yourself." She quickly scanned the room to see if anyone appeared anxious. "I can't dally here too long with you." Her expression suddenly changed. "Hey, you might have your chance!"

"I don't follow you."

"With Mike. You might have a chance to ask him yourself about where he goes."

Rick's face still registered a blank. "I'll need more than that, Jan."

"Next week at the project update."

"You mean the meeting at the station?"

"That's it."

Rick eyed her appraisingly. "How do you know about the project meeting?"

"You're kidding me, right? Like you said before, not much changes around here. The dam project is big news to us, how did you put it, rural folks?"

"And you think this Mike will be there?"

"I do. The Alliance Conservancy has been fairly good at providing news briefs through the local media this past year. Seems like things have been moving ahead."

Rick finally connected the dots. "And you think non camp people will be attending the meeting?"

"Oh you bet I do," she replied. "Alliance has done a decent job of pushing the benefits of the dam removal, but I suspect there will be a few naysayers at your meeting who will have another thing to say. I heard the same woman from last year is leading the meeting next week."

"Sondra," Rick said flatly, his mind recalling rather unpleasant exchanges with the biologist from last summer. "Sondra's back with Alliance?" Jan merely nodded and grinned. "I wonder if Peter knows this?"

Her face suddenly registered distaste. "Haven't seen that uppity colleague of yours here yet. Hell *Erasmus*, you're the first from the camp to darken this door for the summer, though I'm sure the rest of you Bug campers will filter in soon enough now that the great Professor Parsons has arrived."

"Uppity," he repeated, clearly enjoying her characterization.

"Let's just say he's a little full of himself. Don't you even try to defend him. I know you aren't bosom buddies anyway."

"Says who?"

"Says the students, that's who." She smiled broadly. "I have good hearing Rick, and the customers talk.

Students come in and out of here during the summer, and don't think they don't gossip about you all from time to time."

"And let me guess. Peter isn't exactly on the favorites list?"

"Let's just say that the campers aren't always happy about his demeanor."

Rick made a wry face. "That's a good one."

"Don't worry, because I know you're thinking it."

"Meaning?"

"You're safe. The students say you're an ok guy, and somehow, beyond my ability to understand, you have a reputation for making pond scum enjoyable!"

"Algae," he amended.

"Same difference to us folks from the rural side." She didn't give him a chance to respond and changed the subject. "How's you mom?"

"As far as I know she's fine," Rick said. "Haven't been to the lake yet. Hell, I literally just arrived from downstate with a packed car. I'll head first to the station to check in then drive over to see how she's making out with the cottage."

"She been here long?"

"About a month. She likes coming early to get settled in before the rest of the shore arrives. You going to try to come out for a visit? Peach ought to be here soon."

"When's she coming?"

"Could be any day, though it's a little early. Probably not until mid June. You two keep in touch?"

"An occasional message through the winter. She sent a picture of her kids and husband. Looks happy."

Rick nodded encouragingly. "You should come visit. Let me know beforehand if you do, and I'll join you both. It'd be like old times."

She chuckled. "I doubt very seriously that it'd be

like old times, but it would be nice to get together." She gave him a big wink and began to push herself up from the table. "I still think it is pond scum." She laughed again. "Good God Erasmus, we used to make fun of the Bug Camp people in the old days."

He shrugged his shoulders. "Don't hold it against me. It's kinda funny how things turned out."

She turned and walked toward the kitchen to retrieve a waiting order, saying over her shoulder, "Well, you figured out how to spend summers here, so it must suit you." She shook her head and added, "I'll tell the cook you want the regular."

Chapter 2

    The late afternoon sun shone golden across the open field west of the Lake Site Inn, where an unusually wet month had finally made the transition to warmth. Miles leaned against one of the pillars of the entry portico and gazed absently at the swaying tall grasses in the field, wondering if the change in weather would allow the farmers a chance to mow soon. The grass had slowly turned sere in the past week, signaling its readiness, and it rustled softly as it brushed against itself in the shifting breeze.

    A rasping voice called from the kitchen entrance, partially hidden from the main approach. "Donna just called in sick, and we're behind on salad prep."

    Miles hesitated, unsure if the interruption was intended for him. His eyes turned from the field toward the rear corner of the Inn, and he was about to respond when a familiar woman's voice replied. "Move Tracy to assist with frying, and tell the new dessert girl...what's her name again? Tell her that she's doing salads tonight." A mumbled exchange ensued, and he debated whether or not to interfere with his wife's directions, when his attention was diverted as a late model Cadillac pulled leisurely into the lot. He watched as an elderly couple navigated the expanse, parking haphazardly into the first available space so that their left side wheels came to rest over the white line into the adjacent spot. They emerged slowly, both white haired and well dressed, and made their way cautiously to the portico entrance.

"Welcome back, Mr. and Mrs. Henderson," said Miles kindly, straightening his tie and stepping down from the top step to assist the woman as she approached. "We wondered how long it would be until we saw you return up north."

The couple looked about as they neared the steps, taking in the appearance of the Inn as if opening a box of packed away treasures to reacquaint themselves. "Oh Harlan, there's the hummingbird feeders," the wife exclaimed. "And the Geraniums there!"

"Hello Miles," the husband offered, helping his wife up the small steps as Miles descended to take her elbow. "We just arrived yesterday from the Carolinas. Sixteen hours of driving to get here, and Helen says the first place she wants to go is here."

His wife cautiously lifted her leg onto the first step. "This used to be easier. Thank you, dear."

"It's my pleasure Mrs. Henderson."

"Good winter?" asked her husband.

"Long," said Miles. "We had a nasty stretch of snow from January into February, then mostly just cold and dark."

"Which is why we go to Carolina," his wife beamed, having reached the top step and taking Miles's hand into her own as thanks. "We gave up the cold years ago. Can't imagine having to deal with that anymore." She allowed her gaze to sweep the Inn's front and resettled on Miles's face, her eyes slightly moist. "Been coming here for fifty years since we were first married, isn't that right Harlan?"

"Fifty one this summer," he said smiling.

"I'm so glad everything looks exactly the same," she said softly. "Miles, don't you ever change this place."

"You know we wouldn't change a thing." He gestured with one hand toward the entry door. "And why don't you allow me to escort you inside. We've just opened, and you have the choice of seating."

"May we have the table beside the rear picture window?" she asked hopefully. "You know Harlan and I love being able to look out at the feeders you keep and see the lake below. It's all so very pretty and special."

"I think that can be arranged," Miles replied graciously, holding open the door as the pair walked slowly inside. "I'll be along shortly to make sure you are all settled. You'll find our hostess around the corner in the foyer. She'll be happy to take you to your table." He watched as they disappeared around the curving hallway then turned back toward the portico entrance to find his wife approaching from the direction of the back kitchen door.

"How many reservations tonight?" she said curtly.

"Trouble?"

Her expression remained fixed with an air of impatience. "Miles?"

"Four hundred and eighty, mostly early tables."

"Damn," she muttered. "We're going to be short in the kitchen, and I don't know how the hell we'll manage with those numbers." As she finished, another car pulled into the lot. "Why the hell is the early season so full of blue hairs?" A second elderly couple emerged from their parking spot and shuffled toward the entrance.

"I could come back and lend a hand."

Pam critically appraised her husband's clean dress clothes, her face revealing nothing of her private thoughts. "When is Vanholden supposed to be here?"

Miles glanced quickly at his watch then turned his attention to the Woodland Road entrance. "Should be any minute. Said he would stop by on his way back to Harbor but couldn't get here until four o'clock at the earliest."

"And how much is it going to cost us for this visit? I don't see what more can be done about the matter anyway."

"Mitch said he'd been in contact recently with the people from Alliance, and I want to know what he's learned. If there's any possibility of –"

"That's him," she interrupted, both turning their heads to watch as a Jaguar drove purposefully into the lot and parked. "I'll hold down the kitchen, and let's pray it isn't one of those nights."

"It's early, hon. Mostly reservations at this point. Not like July, when they come –"

"No need to tell me that, Miles. Just see what you can learn from Mitch, and come find me if we start getting unexpected walk ins." She turned swiftly and strode back to the kitchen door as he watched her go, his mind recalling Mrs. Henderson's comment about everything staying the same.

"Hi Miles," greeted Mitch simply as he approached with an extended hand. "Sorry I couldn't get away earlier today. I had several unavoidable meetings with clients out in Harbor."

Miles noticed the skin on Mitch's left hand was notably paler as were two lines near his temples where the arms from sunglasses must have been. He wondered if the Harbor meetings actually took place on the golf course at Weque or perhaps Chestnut. "I understand. We've just opened and it has yet to pick up." The pair walked to the front door. "We can meet privately in the bar, and you can tell me what you know."

#

17

Mitch lowered himself onto the teal cushion and let his arms explore the contours of the retro sixties style chair. His eyes took in the similar décor throughout the room. "Where'd you find this stuff?"

Miles surreptitiously eyed the Henderson's in the far room, watching as they pointed toward the large picture window next to the table. "Found it here, that's where." He shifted his gaze to Mitch. "Customers constantly tell us that they love how nothing changes. Well, that's the truth."

"I'm not sure I follow you."

"The Lake Site Inn was built in the late 1940s and opened as a restaurant by the original owners, Kathy and Ken McGowen shortly thereafter." Miles extended his finger and pointed to one of the large windows on the far wall, where in the distance beneath a descending hill, lay the blue expanse of a picturesque body of water. "Lake Kathleen was named for Kathy McGowen."

"They made the lake?"

"The lake was already there, created twenty or thirty years earlier when the town put a dam on the Maple River and used the control flow to initially power a mill. Later, it was used for hydroelectric power, until that failed. Since the 50s, the dam has remained fallow, save for a complete rebuild in the late 60 when it failed."

"Burst, correct?"

"From what I understand, the dam failed, and lake Kathleen emptied rather forcefully down the main stem of the Maple River below." Miles regarded Mitch's calculated expression. "Now, as far as I know there wasn't any loss of life or significant property damage. Thinking as a lawyer, aren't you?" Mitch's mouth formed a thin smile. "However, the discharge altered the Maple downstream. Lots of sediment and erosion spilled down toward Burt Lake. Ruined the fishing for a while, but that eventually came back." Miles stood abruptly. "Excuse me for a moment. Need to say hello to a couple that just entered."

Mitch watched as he vanished through a side door and reappeared moments later, escorting another elderly couple to their waiting table in a far room. He shifted his gaze back to the lake, his mind trying to picture the area beneath devoid of water.

Miles reappeared at the table and took his seat. "Anyway, Lake Site has been open here for nearly seventy years. The original owners sold back in the late seventies to my wife's parents, and they sold it to us thirty years ago." He laughed ruefully and glanced about the room. "The restaurant business isn't easy, you see. Initially, the place was kept going by saving costs, which meant not upgrading the furnishings and decorations. For a while, it bordered on a tacky, I'll grant you. Now, things have come full circle, and people call us retro. You see that couple over there?" he said pointing to the Hendersons. "Typical lifers. They started coming here when Kathy and Ken owned the place, and it looked basically the same as it does today. They're the bread and butter of our sentimental business! Can you imagine if we changed something? We'd certainly hear about it, I can tell you that." Miles pursed his lips as a thought occurred to him. "Shouldn't you already know some of the history of this place, particularly about the lake? I mean, isn't that what you're supposed to be saving?"

"Trying to save," Mitch amended. "If possible, trying to save. And while I am familiar with some of what you described, much of my inquiry involves what may happen next, do you understand?"

"Which is?"

"Miles, I think it's best to be completely frank with you. It doesn't look good."

He leaned back in his chair and exhaled. "There's no way to stop it?"

Mitch shook his head. "I've tried various injunction approaches and made inquiries on your behalf on the basis of potential business hardship. The plain fact is that you no longer have any ownership claim to the lake, and the current owners are within their legal right to have the dam removed."

"And there's nothing that can be done?"

"As I said, it doesn't look promising. The Alliance Conservancy involved Michigan's Department of Natural Resources, the U.S. Fish and Wildlife, Little Traverse Conservancy, and a private engineering firm. The woman that consolidated much of the recent historical research – "

"What was her name?"

"Parker. Dr. Sondra Parker. She's the ecologist that was brought on board to consolidate the research for the Alliance. I'm assuming you know she's the one leading the project update announcement next week at the biological station?"

Miles nodded. "I heard."

"And I assume you're going?"

"Isn't that what we pay you to do?" His expression softened. "Sorry. Yes, either Pam or I will attend the meeting."

"As will I. Early word is that Alliance is pushing to do some additional survey research quickly to bolster their argument about the restoration of the river basin." He gestured toward the window. "You may recall last year they made the case that the lake alters the temperatures for the upper and lower rivers and reduces the natural characteristics for stream fishing. There was push back from some who questioned the expense trade off, given that the temperature data they used for the river was several years old."

Miles shook his head disgustedly. "They want to remove the lake so some stream fishermen will be happy."

"That's a narrow way of looking at it, but it is essentially true. Alliance is also drawing attention to the dam integrity to sway the public. It's over fifty years old and evidently not in good shape. You just described what happened the first time it failed, and Alliance is certainly publicizing that possibility again, though this time there are larger consequences."

"Larger how?"

"Fifty years ago the area along the lower stem was almost remote. Now, there are a few scattered houses along the river. They used to be shacks that got converted into houses as the property values increased. The same is true for the Burt Lake outlet. The river, whether you like it or not, is business, big tourist business, and Alliance is selling this as a win-win for the eco-fishing community."

"Have you heard anything about the timeline?"

"Nothing different than what they proposed last autumn. If they get community buy in, my guess is it's possible they could conceivably do the work this summer."

Miles stared out at Lake Kathleen, imagining it being slowly drained. "There'll be no view at all," he said quietly. "Lake Site Inn without a lake. Just a boggy fen at the bottom of the hill. Hell, we won't even be able to see the river." His gaze returned to Mitch. "It's going to hurt us."

Chapter 3

The truck jostled abruptly as the rear wheel fell into a pothole in the graveled two track, causing the gear in the bed to bang against the floor. Mike glanced apologetically to his passenger. "Sorry about that. I usually remember it when I'm coming in." He slowed the truck as they rounded a bend and approached a small clearing in the woods, the trailing dust backlit from the early evening light through the filter of trees. Mike pointed through the passenger window toward the forest. "There's a small access trail here where we'll go in. It's right through the trees not far there."

"Will I need full waders?"

Mike shook his head. "Nope. Not here. Hips are fine. There are a few pools upstream a ways from here where the river elbows back on itself, and they get a little deep." He nodded encouragingly as he swung the car to the side of the clearing, tucking it under the cover of a large spruce. He shut off the ignition and unbuckled his belt. "Last month you could see the river from here, before the leaves came out and –" He slapped the back of his neck suddenly. "Damn. And before they came out too. We'd better roll up the windows so the skeets don't get in while we're away."

"I didn't bring any bug stuff."

Mike jerked his head to the gear behind them. "I always carry it. We'll need it for at least the next couple of hours till the sun sets. You'll want to spray the back of your neck and shoulders."

"Won't they be attracted to the headlamp?"

Mike opened the door and stood beside, waiting for his passenger to do the same. He examined the logo on the side of the truck, noting several new scratches where the low oak branch on the way in scraped against it. "Dammit," he muttered. "What kind of lamp did you bring?"

His friend joined him at the rear, waiting as Mike opened the hatch and dropped the gate so they could get their gear. "Just a standard lamp? Why?"

"I forgot. You haven't done any night fishing."

"Which is why I brought the lamp, isn't it?"

Mike grabbed a can of bug spray and began to apply it liberally to his upper body. "When things get going later on, and the fish really start to rise, it'll be pitch dark in there." He finished and handed the can to his friend. "Thing is, you need a headlamp with a red light. You have a red light on yours?" His friend merely shrugged as he began to spray himself. "I've got an extra lamp with a red light you're welcome to use. I keep several in the truck for those rare clients who want to go night fishing." Mike reached in and removed a pair of waders, handing them to his friend. "It'll be lights out while we're in the river. You'll use the red light for changing flies or removing one if you get lucky." He found his own waders and began tucking one leg inside, cursing softly as his pant leg began to bunch up. "Dammit." He removed his leg and reached down to pull his socks over the cuff. "Let's try this again."

"The red will be enough?"

"Enough." He finished putting both legs in and wiggled the waders upward. "Your eyes will adjust to the dark a little. There's not much of a moon tonight, and it gets pretty closed in, except for a few pools big enough for the canopy to part. The red's enough to see what you're doing, mostly. Keeps you from blinding yourself and from spooking the fish." Mike put on his vest and grabbed his gear, watching as his friend did the same. "You've never been up this far, have you Dave?"

"Nope. I've been on the lower stem a couple of times down closer to Burt, and never after dark."

Mike chuckled as they closed the gate. "I take most of my clients to the access a little downstream from here. Sometimes we'll park here and go toward the lake."

"Lake Kathleen?"

Mike nodded. "Closer to the lake but still up on the branch." He gestured loosely toward the woods south of the clearing. "There's another access road like this one further on that leads to the branch. And there's a different access, a bigger two track from Robinson that meets the river on the other side." He pointed to a faded sign affixed to the side of old maple near the footpath into the woods, then glanced meaningfully to his friend. "I don't risk taking clients north of here. Certainly not during the daylight, which is when I do most of my guiding."

The pair walked slowly to the path, each making rubbery flopping sounds with their footfalls. In faded letters, the sign read,

Private Property of
University of Michigan
Biological Station
Active Research Area

Dave studied the sign for several moments then turned to meet Mike's eyes. "Then why come here?"

"Because upstream from here is off limits to the public, which means we're more likely to find some big ones in the deep pools."

"What's the Bug Camp doing with this property anyway?"

Mike started up the path, his boots cutting a line through the emerald ferns that nearly obscured the way. "They've got several research projects going on here. At least, that's what I was rather forcefully told last time I got busted for messing about in this section."

"Who the hell's going to catch you out here?"

"That's what I thought," replied Mike. "Except you're likely to find one or more of those scientists doing something here during the day, which is how I got caught." Mike pointed to a spot just ahead, where the path ended abruptly at a large cluster of cedar trees along the shore where the river made a curving elbow upon itself. "There's a thin trail along the shore that begins right..." he said scanning the woods as they approached the river's edge. "Right there." He pointed to what looked like a break within tall grasses that grew next to the cedar where the canopy opened. "See the blue blaze there?" He gestured to a stand of white birch leaning precipitously over the water's edge. "The trail follows the shore all the way up to Robinson Road. Most of the Bug Camp stuff takes place upstream from here at various points on the river. Downstream is public." Mike gestured to the water beyond the cedars. "We'll wade in here and go upstream, hitting a few pools and runs."

"You think we'll be ok here now?"

Mike shrugged. "It's doubtful there'll be anyone out here this time of the day, particularly after dark." He shook his head slowly. "Called the DNR on me last time for trespassing, and they threatened to pull my guide license if I got caught again."

"Look Mike, I'm good if you want to stick to the places downstream."

"Naw. It's ok. Screw it. We're late enough in the day that we can start here where it's still technically public. It's wide enough here we can do some stream casting with the light. Once it gets dark, we'll walk north. It's narrower, and there are several pools I was telling you about. We'll get in there and short cast when the risers come."

"If they come," Dave said.

Mike was first to enter the river, stepping gingerly out from the cedars into the soft sand made by the deposit of the water as it curved, slightly stained with tannin and flowing gently downstream. "There you go," he said, pointing to a mayfly caught on the surface of the water as it passed. "There was a hatch a couple days ago. First real good one of the season."

"Maybe they will come," Dave replied then added jokingly. "Or it's a sign from the Bug Campers. You know, an omen or something not to go upstream."

Mike glanced quickly at his friend, his face darkening. "I get it, ok," he said forcefully.

"Dude, I was only kidding."

"No, not you."

"Then what the hell is wrong? What did I say?"

Mike turned upstream to where the river disappeared around the bend. "If some of those sons of bitches have their way, this whole thing may be screwed."

"What are you talking about? Their research?"

"The river, dammit. I'm talking about the river." He turned his head downstream. "You heard about that project to remove the dam at the lake?"

Dave's face registered confusion for a moment. "The dam below the Lake Site Inn?"

"That's it."

"I heard they want to restore the Maple to its more natural flow. Am I right?"

"That's how it was sold," Mike said disgustedly. "You ever heard of Alliance Conservancy?"

Dave shook his head.

"Well that's the name of the group who's pushing the project to remove the dam and lower the lake to restore the Maple."

"And what does that have to do with the Bug Camp?"

Mike partially ignored the question. "They claim the lake causes the temperature of the lower stem to be too high. They say the Maple is colder upstream on the West and East branches and that the lower part is warmed by the spill off from the lake."

"So?"

"My thoughts exactly!" spat Mike. "*They* are some of the scientists from the Camp Alliance consulted to interpret data and push the project."

"I don't get what the big deal is Mike."

"I'll tell you what the big deal is!" he replied. "I run clients on the East and West. Hell, apart from some sport fisherman who know the area, I've pretty well got a monopoly in these locations. My damn business depends on good fishing in this area."

"And you think the dam removal's going to affect that? I seem to remember hearing that returning the Maple to it's normal flow would be a good thing."

"That's Alliance talking. They've done a fairly good PR job on selling it. Almost had it locked up last year too, until U.S. Fish and Wildlife expressed concerns."

"You've lost me there. Wouldn't Fish and Wildlife want a natural river?"

"Fish and Wildlife told Alliance they wouldn't sign on to the project, because there was no realistic mechanism to prevent predatory fish from moving upstream from the lower stem."

Dave swatted absently at an insistent deer fly around his head. "Still lost me."

"As of now, the fishing's fairly good in the lower stem below the dam. I don't take clients there, because the competition already has itself established."

"You must mean Hidden River."

Mike nodded. "Mostly, and other private guides. Plus, I don't think the fish are all that good there. Sure, there are steelheads that make a run from Burt Lake when the season's right, and people like that, but there's always the issue of the steelies feeding on the young brook trout. Same is true for the lampreys that come up from Burt. Overall the lower stem has more lake fish, and the trout just aren't the same."

"So you mean without the dam, the predators will migrate up into the branches?"

"Exactly. Which means a drop in the brooks upstream, and that's my paycheck."

"I bet the Bug Camp's not ok with that."

"The Bug Camp could give a rat's ass about my livelihood."

"I meant the fish."

"To them a healthy river isn't the same thing as good fishing." Mike began to move to the middle of the river, walking cautiously down a gentle slope of sand until he stood waist deep between the two banks, nearly ten feet from either shore. "Alliance brought in some woman scientist last year to work with the people at the biological station. They did a preliminary proposal and agreed to take up the issue this summer. There's supposed to be some sort of meeting on their campus next week."

"Open to the public?"

Mike nodded. "From what I've heard."

Chapter 4

After the last ice age, as the glaciers retreated across northern Michigan and scoured the landscape below the Laurentian Plateau, they left in their wake large basins of fresh water lakes. With the passage of time, succession transformed the land into what it largely remains today, a near boreal forest of conifers and hardwoods amid rolling terrain composed of sandy soil and boggy lowlands. Of its fifteen miles of shoreline, nearly forty percent of Douglas Lake has been owned by the University Biological Station and remains protected from development, so that apart from the natural evolution of its various ecosystems, the lake appears much as it would have hundreds, even thousands of years ago.

As Rick steered past the station sign and descended the worn asphalt into the border woods, he caught his first glimpse of water through a gap in the pines and pulled suddenly to a stop. He rolled down his window and inhaled, content as the balsam-tinged air filtered into the car. He smiled, thinking of the alchemy at work – how the scents and sounds unique to this place filled him with memories of summer's past. He never failed to value how time seemed to stand still here.

Ahead were several buildings tucked within the woods, their outer pine walls painted brown to blend in with the surrounding landscape, appearing at once resilient to change and slightly dilapidated. The biological station had remained a fixture on the edge of the bay for well over a hundred years.

Initially known as Camp Davis, the first buildings were a series of old tents and ramshackle tin-roofed huts situated on the shore of Fishtail Bay in the southeast corner of the lake. The university acquired the land and adopted it as the Biological Station sometime around 1908, and throughout the ensuing years more buildings and student cabins were added, most set back up the hillside within the cover of the forest. In time, several laboratories for research were constructed as was a modest library, mess hall, administration buildings and a large lecture room. Most of the original tin roofed shacks were still in use each session by attending students, providing each a rustic and cramped living arrangement in the spirit of a north woods summer camp.

Sometime long ago, people began referring to the biological station affectionately as the Bug Camp, and despite its rustic character, it had a strong reputation for conducting teaching and research in several domains within ecology. Resident faculty typically arrived from their host institutions during late May before the first of two summer sessions began. They would often come with their families in tow and stay in one of the more spacious, though still rudimentary, staff houses along the eastern side of the property along the lakeshore.

Students pursued undergraduate and post-graduate studies, including masters and doctoral-level research. The Bug Camp routinely hosted nearly a hundred students per summer and roughly a quarter that number in faculty and staff. Days were typically spent doing fieldwork in and around the lake, including research projects in the surrounding fields, forests and rivers owned by the station.

Rick steered to an upper road and drove several hundred yards to the administration building, where a

"Not you so much as Prima Donna."

Rick smiled knowingly yet refrained from offering any criticism. "How long has he been here?"

"At least three weeks. Brought one of his doctoral students early too, and the pair have been fairly well non stop in the field since."

"Darlene, right?"

"Uh...nope. Darlene called it quits last year."

Rick's eyebrows rose. "He has a new student?"

"That's the truth," Peg said then lowered her voice slightly. "Only seen her a couple times around here since she arrived, and I think she's said maybe two words total. Spends most of her time with Peter in the field, and where else I can't imagine."

Rick smirked conspiratorially. "Can't or won't imagine?"

"The latter, I guess. None of my business, really."

He laughed outright at this, making Peg's eyes widen in surprise. "Peg, I did miss you! None of *your* business. Please. You make everything your business around this place."

Her face quickly shifted from surprise, to mock hurt, to giggles. "Fair enough. I'll give you that. Let's just say that as far as I know," she added, eyeing him meaningfully, "she and Peter are only together in the field." A thought suddenly occurred to her, and she regarded him critically. "You've never brought along a grad student."

"Nope. My home institution doesn't have a Ph.D. program, and besides, I'm happy enough with the session students here."

She nodded in understanding. "That reminds me, you've got thirteen registered for your freshwater class. I've got the roster in the office along with your keys."

Rick's expression was pained. "Please tell me the

rather plump woman in cut off shorts and a faded green T-shirt sat idly in a patch of sunshine on a worn bench. She turned at his approach, her face beaming with recognition as he opened the door.

"As I live and breathe, it's Doc Parsons come back to the north!" She leaned forward and struggled to rise.

"Hey Peggy," he greeted, approaching her uncertainly with his hand outstretched slightly in a half-hearted attempt to initiate a shake.

"A handshake! C'mon Rick, I think we can do better than that." She brushed aside his hand and threw her other arm suddenly around his neck, giving him warm embrace. "How was your winter?" Peg added, retreating a few steps to take him in.

"What can I say, Peg?"

She smiled mischievously. "You could say, winter was long Peg, and I missed you terribly."

Rick laughed and turned his head to the main dirt road fronting the shoreline beneath. "Looks quiet. Not many people here yet?"

Peg shrugged her shoulders. "Most of the students arrive this weekend." She pointed over her shoulder as if through the administration building. "There's a few here already in the upper row."

Rick chuffed. "Let me guess. Peter's?"

"Not exactly," she replied mysteriously. "There are a few international students who wanted to settle in early." She touched her chest and then pointed at him. "Me, now you, Peter of course, Monica – "

"She's running the labs again this year?" he interrupted.

Her mouth turned up in a wry expression. "You know Monica. She bitches and moans about you all. What does she call you? Needy campers, that's it."

"Hey, I'm not that bad!"

housing isn't the same as last year."

"Oh, I know what you mean," she said laughing slightly. "Not to worry. I kept you in the far cottage, same as last year."

"And?"

"And, I put Professor Prima Donna a few cottages away. Told him the one he had last year was being renovated." Her face took on an innocent expression, and she added teasingly, "Wasn't he right next door to you last year?"

Rick pursed his lips. "What are you going to tell him when –"

"Not to worry," she interrupted, reading his train of thought. "We've got a couple spare units out that way anyhow, so I'll just give you the buffer between you and your buddy, and no one but you and I will be the wiser." Peg jerked a thumb toward the building. "C'mon, let's go get your check-in materials." She started walking around the corner toward the office and stopped suddenly, looking over her shoulder. "Oh, and I forgot," her face a mixture of innocence and mischief. "Heather's been in the cottage next to yours for a couple weeks." Her lips formed a smirk.

Rick exhaled forcefully through pursed lips. "I'm sure I don't know what you mean."

Peg laughed. "Why don't you see how things turn out this next month, and then decide?" She winked and turned back toward the office door. "And I suspect you know exactly what I mean. I imagine you'll work things out."

#

Rick opened the screen door and stepped outside, allowing his full attention to take in the view of the bay. Up till now, he'd only had glimpses of the water while he checked in and as he moved his car down from the administration building along the sandy road to the east side where the faculty housing was situated. He'd hastily removed his luggage from the car and dumped it in the small kitchen, impatient for his first real hello.

He walked down the small stony path to the lake's edge and allowed his eyes to scan. Fishtail bay curved gently to the west and then to the north, its shoreline defined by a mixture of conifers and hardwoods that came right to the water's edge, creating a earthy mosaic of varied greens against the foreground of the steel blue water and the bright afternoon sky above. On the far side, the tops of the tallest pines swayed forcefully, and he instinctively glanced beyond the bay to where the lake opened past Grapevine Point. Further out, where the wind came racing down the length of the lake, he saw splashes of whitecaps on large waves moving east toward the sandy shore of big shoal.

A flicker of movement across the bay caught his attention. On the western edge, the square framed aquatic building marked the boundary between the series of camp structures and the forest trails of Grapevine Point. Rick observed as a pair of walkers peeked in and out of view behind the trees, making their way slowly past the outlying buildings and up the main lower road toward the center of camp. He recognized the taller of the two as Peter Cummings, and though Rick was unable to hear their voices from so far away, it was obvious that Peter was agitated about something.

#

"We've only a week! It's rather imperative you collect as much data as possible." Peter clenched a fist at his side and glanced quickly in her direction, gauging a response.

Elise kept her eyes fixed downward on the gravel road and replied submissively, her voice barely above a whisper. "I understand, Dr. Cummings. I'm trying to do my best under the circumstances."

He stopped and faced her squarely. "Well, perhaps you're not trying hard enough."

"I don't see how you expect me to do a thorough survey when the plants have only just begun to distinguish themselves." Her voice raised an octave, though she continued to avoid his gaze. "If we only had another few weeks, once the flowers –"

"Well we don't have a few weeks, do we?" Peter interrupted. "You'll simply have to refine your identification technique without them. Have you revisited the lower site?"

"Several times," she replied, her voice lowering once more. "I've been using the emergent plants there as a known source. I took images when I arrived and again last week when the leaves started to broaden." She finally met his withering gaze. "I'm sorry, but at this stage they look incredibly similar to other species along the target area, and I'm afraid it will be nearly impossible to do a thorough search until the plants develop more or until flowers begin to form."

Peter stepped a few inches closer to her, using his tall frame to intimidate the petite woman. "Need I remind you that my own site is in jeopardy if this restoration goes through as planned."

Elise was tempted to call him an ass right then and there. "There's no need to tell me –"

"And if my primary site goes, it's very well possible that the majority of my funding will be pulled, which means," he paused, tilting his head slightly and regarding her down the length of his nose, "that you will have to search for a new doctoral mentor." He waited several moments to allow his words to set in, challenging her to meet his gaze.

"What would you like me to do?" she said resignedly, still keeping her eyes lowered to the ground. She waited cautiously for his reply, fixing her concentration on a small inchworm that ambled across the stony drive beneath her feet.

He inhaled slowly. "I need to continue monitoring my site on the East Branch. You're right about the flowers. Some of my upper stems are beginning to show signs of budding, and it's rather critical I measure the surrounding data points at this stage."

"What about getting one of the students who just arrived to –"

"To what?" he said almost accusingly. "To assist you? Me?" He shook his head disgustedly. "Few of the students ever have sufficient experience in plant morphology to even begin to help. We haven't the time to train a new person." He threw his hands up in the air. "Weren't you listening before? I need something within a week!" His voice became even more strident. "Ms. Parker?"

Elise's attention had shifted to the east side of the camp, where she examined what she thought was a person standing near the shore. "Looks like someone's arrived."

Peter jerked his head in that direction, and his eyes narrowed. "Oh good God. That must be Erasmus."

She thought surely she must have misheard him. "Who did you say?"

"I said that's Erasmus. Dr. Erasmus Parsons."
"Is he faculty?"
"Yes. Actually a local of sorts."
"Local as in, well … from here local?"
"Not exactly. He spent his summers here growing

up. Family has a place on the north side of the lake."

Elise considered his reaction. "What about asking for his help?"

"Erasmus! Lord, no. He's an algae phycologist, not a botanist. And frankly, I find him a bit of a provincial."

Again, she considered calling him a prick or at the very least pointing out to him that a phycologist is likely knowledgeable about fundamental plant morphology. She smirked as another thought occurred to her.

"Well, what do find so amusing? I see that expression on your face!"

"Erasmus, that's what."

"Meaning?"

"A botanist. Er...sorry. A phycologist named Erasmus. Don't you think that's a bit funny?"

"I know well enough that *he* doesn't think so. Prefers to be called 'Rick' rather than Erasmus."

"But surely it can't be just a coincidence? I mean, talk about your name of destiny. Can you imagine being named Erasmus? It almost locks you into a career in plants."

"Algae!" he corrected pompously.

"Fine, algae," she repeated.

"And I doubt seriously that his parents took any such thing into consideration. Frankly, I couldn't care less. The fact remains that he will be of no use to us, which leaves us with a deadline." Peter took several steps ahead on the road and turned once more to regard her. "I suggest you get an early start tomorrow and work your way up the branch, beginning on the east shore of Lake Kathleen. Pay particular attention to where the East discharges, and follow the flow on both sides."

"What about the West Branch?"

"East first, given that I already have a positive site up stream. If we –"

"By 'we' you mean 'me'," Elise thought.

" - can find another specimen somewhere along the East, I think that will strengthen the case. If not, we'll hope for something along the West." He waited to see if she had any reply. "Of course, if you discover anything, try calling me. I'll have my cell at the site, but the coverage is next to nothing." With that, he turned once more and continued onward, leaving her alone in the middle of the road.

#

Rick watched as Peter left his companion and walked the remaining distance toward the faculty housing. For a moment, he worried Peg had lied to him about the living arrangements, and he began to stew about a summer of having Professor, what did she call him? Professor Prima Donna, that's it - Professor Prima Dona living right next door. Instead, Peter turned to the front door of a cottage three down from Rick's and disappeared inside.

The young woman had turned from the street and gone toward the administration building, leaving the main road completely empty, save for the tin can student houses on the lake side and the various brown campus buildings on the other. For a moment, Rick was reminded of a scene from an old western in which the camera pans the length of the abandoned town. Soon enough the remaining faculty and students would arrive and populate the campus, transforming it into a strange combination of academic institution and summer camp, with a tinge of a Grateful Dead atmosphere.

Rick's phone suddenly chimed a message. "Are you here?" read the text sent from across the lake. He smiled, admiring that she'd taken so easily to modern communication. He quickly tapped a reply. "Just arrived and checked in. Very quiet here for now. I'll stop by tomorrow morning, ok?" He hit the send button and waited several minutes as the phone indicated a reply was being written.

"Ok. Glad you're here. Pick up gallon of milk at Van Store if you come that way."

"Will do," he answered, pocketing the phone as the back porch slider of the cottage next door opened softly. A slender brown haired woman in jeans and a long-sleeve white T-shirt emerged. She glanced initially to the left toward the shoreline and campus, saying softly with a lilting Irish accent, "Is anyone there?"

Rick had forgotten how truly lovely she was. "Hi Heather."

This clearly startled her. "Jeepers!" she shouted (which wasn't much more than a slightly raised voice), turning quickly in his direction. "You nearly scared the wits out of me."

He held his hands out in front to offer amends. "So sorry. Thought I should say something, rather than wait until you happen to turn around and see me just standing here."

In an instant, her eyes widened in recognition then softened. "You're living next door?" Rick nodded. "That's right," she continued. "You had that cottage last year." Her mouth turned up in concentration. "And this one was Peter's, right?"

"Right again. Peg's put him down a few places this summer."

Heather stepped from the porch and moved slowly to where he stood in the path. She stopped short and eyed him hesitantly. "All right if I give you a proper hug hello?"

The awkward exchanges from last summer immediately played out in his mind. "Sure." He stepped forward as she put a tentative arm around him, lingering a little too long for comfort. Her perfume smelled something of vanilla. "How long have you been here?" Rick said, moving back so as not to give the wrong impression. "I assume you were one of the first to arrive?"

She nodded and then spoke in that soft, musical accent Rick found so alluring. "I came immediately after our finals week was over at Bowdoin. Didn't stay for the graduation." She saw a questioning look on his face. "My department understands, especially this year since April was so warm."

"You must have been here by yourself for a couple weeks."

"Not entirely," she replied. "The director's been here since February, and there's been some activity around campus with maintenance." She glanced momentarily out toward the water, distracted by a pair of Mergansers that swam idly along the shore. "Mostly, I've been doing my data on the Grapevine sites and along the lower basin near the springs." She turned once again and met his eyes. "Several species started pollinating early, so I had to be here, you see?"

"Are you on your own?"

Her eyes widened slightly, and her cheeks took a slight flush. Rick immediately regretted the question. "What did you say?" Heather said softly.

"What I meant was, were you able to bring a graduate student from Bowdoin with you to help?"

If she was embarrassed by his retreat, she didn't reveal it. "No. Just me, until the students arrive soon." She studied his face carefully to see if he may have intended something else. "I'm teaching the intro botany course this first session, and I'll be able to coax one or more of the students into a thesis project that dovetails with my own research. At least I'll have some help with the midsummer plants." She smiled subtly. "And what about you?

Anyone?"

Rick thought he'd better go carefully. "No, it's just me. We don't have a graduate program downstate anyway, so I'll do the same as you."

"No hold overs from last summer?"

He shook his head. "Both Alana and Marco finished their theses last year. A student who's coming from Michigan State for the first session contacted me. She's interested in climate change and said she wants to work with me doing collections." Rick shrugged. "We'll see. There are always a handful of students willing to get wet. I suspect we'll both have enough help in a week or so."

Heather turned her head and glanced toward his car. "Need any help unpacking?"

"I'm fine for now. I dumped most of my stuff in the living room only twenty minutes ago. It won't take me that long to settle in."

"And then what?" Her expression gave away nothing.

"I guess we've got a couple days. Tomorrow morning I'm going over to the north shore to see how my mom's getting along. I'd also like to head into town to get some groceries and some wine. You have plans?"

"For the weekend? Nothing special. And I already have groceries." She hesitated a moment as a slight smile played on her lips. "And wine."

Now it was his turn to act neutral. "Is this an invitation?"

She laughed softly. "Yes it is. Tell you what. I'll grab my bottle of wine, and you go check out one of the pontoons from the aquatics building. Did you get your building keys?"

He nodded and fished around in the front pocket of his pants, finding the keychain Peg gave him earlier. "How am I going to log this?"

"I seriously doubt anyone will be monitoring boat usage now. The logbook is probably not even out yet. Just get a pontoon, and come pick me up in fifteen minutes from the main dock." With that, she turned and headed back toward her screen door, leaving him standing there, wondering if this was such a good idea.

Chapter 5

Heather sat in the bow on one of the cushioned benches as the boat cleared the shadows from Grapevine Point and made its way into open water. Rick marveled how the forest of cedar and spruce lined the shoreline so thickly, particularly here where the trunks came directly to the water's edge. "The lake's high," he said loudly above the engine noise. She glanced to the shore and watched the trees as they passed quickly by. She turned to him and said in a raised voice, "Slow down here, will you?"

He eased back the throttle and the boat settled into a leisurely cruise. "What is it?"

She smiled and withdrew a bottle of wine from a soft cooler beside her. "Nothing. I'd rather we putt along like this so we can hear each other." She fished out a tool from inside the bag and deftly twisted free the cork. "It's amazing, you know. Take a look at that." She pointed with the hand holding the opener toward the south shore. "It's pristine. Unspoiled." She surveyed the shore in both directions for hundreds of yards then returning her attention to him. "Do you think it looked like that thousands of years ago?"

Rick moved the throttle to neutral and turned off the engine, allowing the boat to glide slowly ahead in the shallows. The water here was calm and reflected the yellow sand beneath. "Need help?" he asked. Heather shook her head as she removed two glasses from the cooler and poured them each a little white wine.

She raised her glass to clink his in a toast. "Welcome back."

"Here's to another summer." Rick nodded his head toward the shore. "It's funny your asking that."

"How come?"

"Because I spend most of my time with students collecting data either out in the middle of the water or along the shore, and I sometimes wonder the same question when we look into the woods."

"You mean whether they've changed?"

"Sort of. I mean, I know the trees have gone through major successions over the past several hundred years. And I'm sure you could tell me exactly how the diversity of pollinators have shifted, so I realize my question's a little silly." She eyed him curiously as he wondered whether to continue. "I grew up here." He turned to his right and gestured toward a far shore near a rounding point, "Actually, over there. You know I spent summers here as a kid?" Heather nodded. "Been coming ever since, and what never fails to amaze me is how things don't seem to change all that much."

She smiled. "Tell me what the station was like when you were younger."

"The Bug Camp!" Rick laughed. "We always thought they were nerds. It's the truth, I'm ashamed to admit it. A bunch of us yahoos ran around together on the north shore, and we'd take the boats down the lake toward Fishtail to go swimming or just to mess around, and we'd see the camp students out on their pontoon boats or along the sedge ponds doing goofy science stuff." He laughed. "Go figure all these years later I ended up joining them."

"And your, what did you call them? Yahoo friends? What would they think?"

"Well, most of us are still in touch. We overlap a

little during the summer, and I try to go see them at the old haunts. Most of them ended up pretty much just like me. In one way or another we became the kind of people we used to make fun of." He grinned at her. "I guess we just grew up."

"Which means that some things do change here after all, don't they?"

Rick watched as the sun reemerged from a passing thin cloud, first illuminating the distant water to the west. He pointed toward the narrow gap between the south shore and the tip of the island that jutted outward into the lake. "Look how it's backlit through there."

Heather's eyes followed the shoreline toward the island, lingering a moment where the private cottages began as the bay turned in upon itself. She looked through the gap, searching the tree line of the far shore. "Is that where the Maple River begins?"

Rick followed her gaze and nodded. "It's near where you can see those trees way off in the distance. Just a little to the left, behind that small point where the land gets kinda boggy." He turned back to her. "You've never been there?"

Heather shook her head. "I imagine you've collected there."

"I have, though it's been a few years. Why do you ask?"

"Well, I guess I was thinking about what you just said. You know, about nothing changing. We heard enough about the Maple last year from Alliance, and I wondered if what they wrote was accurate."

"You mean about the river not being adversely affected."

"I suppose. Do you think –." She stopped and looked at him suddenly. "You *are* going to the update next week, aren't you?"

"Yeah, I'll be there. I imagine the whole camp will attend. In fact, there's likely to be a fair turnout from the surrounding community."

Heather looked at him curiously. "The community? You think there'll be trouble?"

Rick shrugged. "Tough to say. Sondra rather smoothly – "

"That's her name! I kept thinking it was Sandy or Stephanie." Her eyes narrowed, and she pursed her lips. "I only spoke with her a few times while she was gathering information last summer. Actually, she mostly spoke *to* me. She sure didn't ask me for my professional point of view. I didn't care for her all that much."

"She's alright I guess. A little overbearing for my taste. I imagine Peter feels rather strongly about her."

Heather laughed and rolled her eyes. "Peter feels strongly about everything and everybody. What was his beef again exactly?"

"Well, that's why I think the update might get a little interesting, and in this instance, I have to admit I think Peter raised some important concerns. Sorry," he added, seeing a slight look of confusion on her face. "I forgot you'd already gone last August when Sondra presented her report." Rick noticed the water had changed to a lighter shade of yellow, and he glanced over the side. "Oops. We've drifted in a little too much." He started the engine and motored slowly from shore until they came to the drop off, lined with thick patches of macrophytes and streaming bits of chara algae. He disengaged the engine once more and turned the key. "I suspect Alliance knew there'd be a few gremlins with the dam removal, which is likely one of the reasons why they enlisted the Bug Camp as a primary ally in the first place."

"Are you suggesting what I think?"

"Not exactly. It makes sense Alliance would want

to bring in our group to support the dam removal. We get tapped for our experience, we add a stamp of approval, and we are offered a unique opportunity to do some research on river restoration. It all seems like a win-win, right?"

Heather nodded. "So what's the big deal?"

"Well, I suspect they knew there'd be some resistance to the project. Some of it was predictable, like the concerns raised by the U.S. Fishing and Wildlife and the fear from local property owners."

"I read about the lamprey concerns in the report."

He smiled. "Nicely done. I see you didn't just check out entirely after last July."

Her voice lilted softly in mock hurt. "Be nice. Don't you dare assume that a pollen scientist isn't interested in the river basin or political dynamics for that matter."

"Didn't mean to imply anything of the sort," he chided. "And, yes. I think the lamprey issue is legitimate. At least, I imagine there's a bunch of sport fisherman who do."

"You think they understated the possibility of predatory fish?"

Rick shook his head. "No, I wouldn't go that far. I think it's just a big unknown. I give Sondra credit for being up front about it. Well," he laughed, "she would have been accused of negligence had she not discussed it." Rick glanced again through the gap at the distant shore. "I've got a buddy who does quite a bit of fly fishing up and down the Maple. He goes mostly below the dam in the main stem, though occasionally he does dabble in one or the other branches upstream from Lake Kathleen. He's described to me what I've read elsewhere about the river. There are more predatory fish like lamprey and migratory steelheads in the main stem, and they do affect the overall quality of the small trout stock."

"They come up from Burt Lake into the Maple."

"Yep. Actually, they come from Huron through the waterways and eventually into Burt. Then up into the Maple where it spills out. They and other lake fish go up the river to spawn and also prey on the cold water trout."

"But there's still trout in the lower stem."

"Oh yeah. It's stocked yearly by the DNR, and there's enough despite the predatory fish. It's the upper river branches, the East and West above the dam that are at issue. The dam prevents the predators from gaining access. According to my friend, the fishing in the branches is far better for trout."

"And what about the properties on Lake Kathleen?"

"The only real property to speak of is the Lake Site Inn. They've been around a while. You ever eaten there?"

She nodded. "Couple of times last summer. Kept getting sick of hearing people saying it's the best fried chicken for a thousand miles, so I finally went."

"And?"

Heather raised her eyebrows and gave him a matter-of-fact expression. "I went more than once."

"Well, the Lake Site Inn kind of has a vested interest in their panoramic view, don't you think? I mean, the name doesn't really make sense if the dam goes and lake gets drained."

"And you were saying before about Peter?"

"Yeah, Peter. I imagine Alliance didn't anticipate that issue."

"Which do you mean, the issue of Peter, or the issue of his concern?"

Rick laughed. "Good one. Both, I guess. And in this case I have to side with Peter. In fact, after the meeting last summer I made a point of telling him that."

"And I imagine your show of support just bolstered his ego."

It was Rick's turn to look contrite. "I think that's sarcasm, but it's a little difficult to tell. Peter doesn't exactly need his ego boosted, particularly from this little pond scum scientist."

"Pond scum scientist?"

"Yeah," he laughed again. "I got called that earlier today from an old friend. She does it just to make sure I don't get too full of myself as a Bug Camp nerd." Rick gestured toward the soft cooler. "How about a refill."

Heather removed the bottle and handed it to him. "Peter's mostly invasive species work. I don't remember reading anything about a potential effect – "

"Peter's interested in both invasive *and endangered* species. Mostly the former, I grant you. But he also has been tracking climate change data on the latter."

Her voice raised a little as the connection dawned on her. "You mean the Monkeyflower."

"Bingo," he replied. "That could be a sticky wicket." His mouth gave a wry expression. "Isn't that an Irish saying?"

Her face showed disapproval. "British, not Irish.

"Same difference." he quipped.

"I'll ignore that, *Erasmus*."

"As will I. Ok, the Monkeyflower. Yes, that could be interesting. There's a known population below the dam near the outflow where the main stem begins. Here's where I think Sondra was either a little sloppy or she withheld some key information."

"I seem to recall her mentioning the Monkeyflower in the report."

"She did, but she also refrained from highlighting a key aspect about that particular group."

"Oh, I remember now!" Heather interjected. "Of

the known locations of the Monkeyflower...wait, how many are there?"

Rick closed his eyes as he tried to recall. "Eight, I think. There are two along the south shore of the U.P., one near some wetlands around Harbor Springs, two east of Sturgeon Bay in the springs area, two close to the north shore of Burt, and the last is near the outlet of Lake Kathleen."

"I knew it was endangered, but only eight? Peter brought me viable pollen last year from the dam. I've got a little sample for the station collection in a glass vial and some on mounted slides."

"And that's the sticky wicket," he repeated, seeing her guarded reaction to his reuse of the phrase. "Only the location at the dam produces flowers with viable pollen. All the other sites reproduce without it."

"No flowers?"

"Oh, they bloom alright, but they don't produce much pollen, if at all. Any reproduction is done by rooting of broken stems in the wet areas where it grows, and this is pretty rare." Rick tilted his head and eyed her seriously. "The dam patch is known to produce both pollen *and* seeds. Nobody is sure why, but it's a pretty rare thing."

"Even Peter doesn't know why?"

"I don't think so. He takes groups of students to the site to monitor all sorts of data about the soil and water chemistry. You'd have to ask him yourself. The fact is, the dam may very well play a critical role in creating the unique niche for that particular patch. Sondra's report tended to gloss over the potential ramifications."

Heather exhaled audibly. "I see what you mean about a sticky wicket."

Rick chuckled. "And there's more. Late last summer, after the Alliance report, Peter identified another patch of Monkeyflower in an area along the East Branch."

"Seriously? With flowers?" She hesitated, realizing the answer to her own question. "No, wait. There wouldn't have been any. They flower in June."

"Peter was able to I.D. the patch using basal morphology. It's pretty distinctive. It's a confirmed location, which would make it number nine for known sites in the entire world, all in this area."

"So let me guess, he's waiting to see if this new site produces flowers over the next week."

"I imagine so. He's got a new graduate student with him –"

"Yeah, I've seen her. Haven't spoken to her."

"Peg says he and the new student have been in the field almost non stop since they arrived. I bet he's collecting all sorts of data on the new site and waiting to see if it blooms."

"And if so, you think it'll impact the proposal?"

"Peter will certainly argue so. At least, it will give him leverage to sustain his site."

"The new site?"

"That and the fact that he does most of his research along the upper east branch. He has a vested interest in keeping things just the way they are."

"And you?" Heather said. "How do you feel about the river restoration?"

Rick noticed the boat had again drifted into the shallow water. He started the engine and barely engaged the throttle, setting a slow course to cruise along the edge of the drop off. "I guess it doesn't matter one way or the other to me. Most of my funded research takes place around the lakes, not in the rivers. And honestly, I look at it that the restoration will open up new opportunities, if I want them. Or at the very least, I'll have a handful of potential projects for any incoming students." He noticed Heather had drawn her legs up on the bench to keep warm.

The sun was still ten degrees above the Western horizon, and Rick laughed softly as he checked his watch.

She looked at him curiously.

"It's been a long day, and yet, look where the sun is." He pointed to the sky above the line of trees along the island's ridge. "There's still over an hour until sunset, and it's nearly nine o'clock!"

"Let's hope it's a long summer," she said wistfully. "And I suppose we'll be seeing more of each other, now that we're officially next door neighbors."

He laughed warmly and threw her an old towel that was draped on the back of the captain's chair. "Here, use this as a blanket." He turned his head and nodded back the way they'd come. "Let's go back to the camp."

"You dodged my comment there," she added shyly.

"No," he replied evenly, his eyes scanning the shoreline. "Didn't dodge it. Just considering it." Then he turned directly toward her. "It's a very small camp, you know."

Heather nodded and laughed too. "Then let's head back and enjoy the calm before the rest arrive."

Chapter 6

The lights flickered briefly in the Gates hall, signaling to the crowd to take their seats and settle down. The lecture room was filled to capacity, and when it had become obvious they would need more chairs than what the room was designed to accommodate, Peg solicited several of the attending students to go get folding chairs from the dining hall next door. These were taken rather quickly, and with the late arrivers who resorted to standing in the back of the room, the entire gathering was claustrophobic and incendiary.

Sondra leaned into the podium microphone and rather tersely commanded. "Could I have someone help me reconnect my laptop to the LCD projector?"

Peg, who was relegated to having to stand in the back row (and clearly irritated that two students she'd charged with IT assistance were seated and oblivious) shouted, "Ryan. Ryan!" She gave him a withering look and nodded her head forcefully toward Sondra in the front.

In the momentary lull, Rick surveyed the crowd, finding the usual suspects from the camp dispersed throughout the room. Peter and his graduate student sat on the right side in the middle of the audience. Monica and David not coincidentally chose the left. Where was Heather? He spotted her a few rows up from his own, her attention turned to one of the new students seated beside her, dressed in a tie dye shirt and jeans just like from the seventies. In the front row sat two individuals from the

Alliance Conservancy. Rick recognized them from the presentation last summer. Next to them was someone from the DNR, Patty or something like that. Beside her sat the regional agent for the Fish and Wildlife Services, dressed in what Rick regarded as a rather impressive green uniform. Sondra stood behind the podium in a crisp white button down shirt and grey slacks, her black hair pulled back too tightly in a pony tail, giving her face a decidedly witchy countenance. Well, perhaps he wasn't being fair.

Peppered within the audience were some local faces he knew. There were many others he didn't, including a uniformed police officer with a sidearm positioned by one of the near entry doors to the hall. She was petite and rather pretty he thought, and he allowed his eyes to linger too long when he found her staring back at him with cool appraisal.

With Sondra's technical problem resolved, she signaled to another student to dim the room lights. "Welcome everyone," she began in an overly loud voice, irritating Peg on two fronts.

"She's welcoming *us* to our own station," Peg whispered to one of the administration staff that stood beside her.

"I know that while many of you were in attendance last year when I presented the initial report from Alliance, I can see there are new faces here this evening, and so I'd like to begin with some introductions."

Rick glanced again to the uniformed officer, who continued to scan the audience impassively.

"I am Dr. Sondra Parker, and I am the lead collaborator from the Alliance Conservancy."

Even from several rows away, Rick clearly heard Peter chuff softly under his breath, "Some collaborator."

"Seated before me here are representatives from the various organizations that in one way or another have been instrumental in helping us to move forward with the restoration of the Maple River." She gestured to a person to her right. "Douglas Field is the Natural Resources Director for the Little Traverse Bay Band of Ottawa Indians. Next to him is Phillip Kolniak of the U.S. Department of Fish and Wildlife. Then we have Patricia Alexander from Michigan's Department of Natural Resources. Steve Wilmer and Caroline Cox are executives from the Alliance Conservancy, and finally we have Charles Henderson, whom I'm sure most of you recognize as the Director of the University of Michigan Biological Station." Several individuals within the crowd initiated a half-hearted applause, which then encouraged others to join.

Sondra used a hand-held clicker to project an aerial image of the Maple River Basin. "Last year I summarized the work done to determine the feasibility of restoring the Maple River, which as you see is represented here in the aerial photograph. Alliance contracted me to act as the point person for gathering data on the benefits and potential risks for the removal of the concrete dam presently existing at the southern part of Lake Kathleen." Sondra advanced the slide to display a close-up view of the spillway from the lake, leading downhill toward the main stem of the Maple below Woodland Road. "Allow me to briefly review the proposal I made here last year."

Rick's attention was diverted by Jan, who sat a few rows in front of him and had turned around to face him. She was waving to get his attention with one hand and pointing down her row with the other. Slightly confused, he gave her a quick wave of his own and turned his eyes in the direction she indicated. On the other side of the room sat Miles Kirnan from the Lake Site Inn, his expression neutral as he listened patiently to Sondra's opening remarks.

"For over a hundred years, the flow of the Maple

River has been interrupted by the construction of a dam, which resulted in the creation of Lake Kathleen. The original dam, built in the early nineteen hundreds, was used to power a mill and then subsequently a hydroelectric generator. That dam failed in 1952 and was ultimately rebuilt in 1967 to its present structure. Several years ago, the current dam was deemed in desperate need of repair in order to minimize the possibility of another failure. It was at that time several parties, including the organizations seated before me, considered the alternative of removing the Lake Kathleen dam in order that the Maple River be restored to its more natural condition."

Sondra returned to the initial slide depicting the aerial view of the river, and she used a pointer to highlight various locations as she continued. "The watershed of the Maple River is approximately 168 square miles, encompassing the origin locations for the East and West Branches, the downstream flow through lake Kathleen, and the lower stem as it meanders roughly southeasterly through a forested riparian corridor toward its ultimate discharge into Burt Lake. Though the Maple is classified as a relatively cold stream, since it is fed both by the waters of Douglas Lake through the East Branch and through various springs within both branches and within the lower stem, the presence of Lake Kathleen artificially divides the river into two zones."

"As we reported, the upper branches are notably colder than the lower stem, with Lake Kathleen acting as a heat sink and elevating the temperature of the discharge downstream by as much as a six degrees, depending on the season. As a result, the upper branches are classified as a cold streams, and the lower stem is considered cold transitional, the latter affecting the quality and quantity of stream fish that are sustained. We used the data from Michigan Department of Natural Resources to document the historical temperature differences at various locations along the branches and the lower stem. This data also included measurements of fish biomass and population counts within these areas, documenting the likely differences between the two zones on viable stream fish populations, both in terms of fish density and individual biomass."

Rick saw Jan's head jerk to the other side of the room when she heard the distinctively husky voice of Mike Pritchard interrupt. "Isn't the data you used nearly ten years old, if not more so!"

The crowd as one turned to see who had spoken. Sondra remained perfectly composed, deciding whether or not to invite the unwelcome participant to introduce himself. "Ah, yes that is correct," she replied evenly. "In fact, this is one of the principal reasons why I have returned this season, per Alliance's directive. State funding for the project was contingent on our conducting contemporary temperature measurements along various locations comparable to what was done years ago."

"And I suppose you think you'll have similar results?" Mike said rather challengingly.

Sondra's eyes narrowed slightly. "We will measure the river in several locations both above and below the dam, fifteen sites altogether, including in the upper and lower portions of both the East and West Branches. This work will commence immediately."

At her mention of the words "East Branch," Rick glanced over to see Peter's reaction, and he wasn't disappointed. Prima Donna visually straightened in his chair, considered saying something of his own to the speaker, and then began whispering animatedly to the young woman seated next to him.

"What about the lamprey?" shouted someone nearer the front, hidden from Rick's view.

Sondra turned to the man seated before her. "I'd like Phillip to address that issue, if you don't mind Phillip?" Sondra nodded encouragingly to him, and as the man rose and began to approach the podium, she added, "Of course the lamprey issue was raised as a legitimate concern last year, and our funding was also jeopardized by the reluctance of the Fish and Wildlife to endorse the dam removal. I'd ask Phillip to comment on the status of the lamprey issue and the position of their department at this time. Phillip?"

Henry Thoreau. That's what Rick thought as Phillip Kolniak took to the podium and gazed at the audience. Phillip looked exactly like the historical photographs of a late thirties something Thoreau, with dark hair and a slightly unkempt beard, a dark jacket over an ironically clean and pressed white shirt. The voice, however, didn't match what Rick thought should be a New England dialect. Phillip Kolniak was born and bred in northern Michigan and infused his words with that unique mixture somewhere between Minnesota and Canada.

"Thank you Sondra. Last year, our group did not endorse the removal of the Lake Kathleen dam on the basis of the potential for predatory fish to migrate further up the Maple River. Presently, the lower stem is subject to various lake fish that prey upon the smaller stock of brown, brook and the occasional rainbow trout, certainly affecting the quality of sport fishing in this area. Were the dam removed, it is possible that such fish as the Sea Lamprey would take advantage of further migration into the West and East branches, where they would gain access to thus far undisturbed pools and runs. It would, and let me stress again, possibly, affect the young stock of trout in these locations."

"However," he continued, "we've been encouraged by the results of data shared with us by the Alliance

Conservancy, that show how sterilization release programs conducted in other locations similar to what we experience through the Huron and Cheboygan waterway basins, can effectively control Sea Lamprey numbers. We now believe that it will be possible to release male sterile fish in sufficient quantities prior to their migration so that if and when they do migrate into the lakes and river basins, they will not produce viable sperm during the seasonal spawn. And hence, no offspring that would otherwise prey upon the trout population prior to their downstream return to the big lakes."

"But that's certainly no guarantee!" shouted Mike, causing the crowd once again to turn in his direction. "And there would certainly be increased predation from the upstream migration prior to the spawn!"

"True," replied Phillip. "But it would likely be minor, compared to the downstream event."

"Thank you, Phillip," Sondra interrupted hastily, giving him a patronizing hand on the shoulder while gesturing with her other that he retake his seat. She then turned to the crowd, and raised both hands. "And so there you have it."

Good Lord, thought Rick. Was she really going to try to summarize at this juncture?

"At this point, the state is withholding final approval until we provide them with supplemental temperature data and – "

"Excuse me, Dr. Parker," interrupted Peter, as he stood upright among the seated crowd around him.

"Yes, Peter?" she replied neutrally.

Rick rolled his eyes. In stark contrast to Phillip Kolniak's comforting local manner, Peter exuded almost a Kennedy-esk blue blood persona, certainly amplified to set him apart. "For those of you who don't know me, I'm Dr. Peter Cummings, a faculty member here at the Biological

Station."

"Yes, Dr. Cummings," Sondra amended, her emphasis now placed on his title.

If Peter was mollified by her readdress, he gave no indication. "My research examines the effect of climate change on the population dynamics of both invasive and endangered species, principally plants, though not exclusively so."

Jan turned around again and made eye contact with Rick. "Nerds" she mouthed, smiling then as she pointed first at Peter then directly at him.

Rick knew Peter was clearly in his element, with an attentive audience that he believed hung on every word he was about to utter. What he didn't understand was that most just wanted him to get to the point and be done with it.

"It is well known within botanical circles..."

"Good grief," Rick thought.

"... that one of the more rare annual wildflowers, *Mimulus michiganensis,* or by its common name the Michigan Monkeyflower, only grows in a handful of locations here within a roughly thirty mile radius of the Maple River basin."

Sondra was beginning to lose patience. "Dr. Cummings, our group attended to the importance of the Monkeyflower as an endangered species of consideration in the report last year."

"Ah, but I think you omitted a rather key aspect from full disclosure," he rebutted, clearly pleased by the look of contriteness on her face. Peter turned to face the audience. "The Monkeyflower is rather peculiar in that for reasons not clearly understood, it rather rarely puts forth viable pollen and as such refrains from reproducing by seed. The plant can propagate by cutting, which has been known to occur, but again, this is rare. Monkeyflower requires rather narrow conditions for growth, largely that of cold, mucky waters which are spring fed and slightly acidic. Again, for reasons not entirely known, there is only one location of the Monkeyflower in which the plant produces blossoms with both viable pollen and actual seeds."

"I assure you, Dr. Cummings," Sondra interjected forcefully. "The consortium that advised the Alliance Conservancy seriously considered the endangered status of the location to which you are referring, and this was documented in the report last year."

Peter stood his ground, shaking his head emphatically. "With all due respect, Dr. Parker, I think your group made an oversight into the potential delicacy of this particular location."

"I do not appreciate what you are implying. Dr. Cummings," she said evenly.

"Be that as it may, your report failed to mention the reproductive status of this unique patch, which certainly elevates the risk of moving forward with the dam removal." Peter again turned to the rest of the audience. "Yes, Alliance did report that Monkeyflower grows below the dam basin. However, they did not highlight that the site below the dam is the *only* known location to produce pollen and seed. What Alliance cannot guarantee, what no one could guarantee is whether or not the restoration of the river, which would undoubtedly alter the water and soil chemistry of the surrounding area, will impact the reproductive strategy or even the viability of this particular site." Peter shifted again to face Sondra directly. "There's more. I have identified another heretofore unknown site of Monkeyflower growing in the upper stretch of the East Branch, within the border of the property of the Biological Station. Though it is too early to discern if the plant will produce viable pollen, I can confirm that new bud growth has taken place and that flowers are forthcoming."

"And I suppose this new site you've discovered is conveniently within the area bounded by your principal funded research?" she asked archly.

"I will not reply to that implication," he said curtly. "Rather, I will say it is clear the Monkeyflower now has *two* known sites within the direct path of the Maple, and these sites may be contingent on the status of the existing condition of the river."

Patricia Alexander stood and turned to face the audience. "I'm Patty Alexander from the DNR. Of course, we are concerned about the status of the Monkeyflower, though we are confident from our hydrological engineer that the dam removal should have a relatively low impact on the soil and growth condition for the existing patch."

"I should like to see how that was determined," demanded Peter, still standing before the crowd.

"And, I assure you that the DNR will work closely with you, Dr. Cummings, to consider your findings of this new site, while we await the data collection that Dr. Parker anticipates doing on the temperature gradients over the next few weeks."

Peter nodded curtly, satisfied that he'd introduced a sufficient wrinkle into the project to jeopardize its progress. He took his seat and began whispering softly to Elise.

Sondra continued. "At this time, I'd like to invite any other comments or questions about the status of the project."

Jan chuckled, clearly amused at the academic sparring that just took place. "Have you gathered any data on the Lake Site Inn?" she asked pointedly, her face smiling suggestively.

Sondra didn't immediately understand the nature of her question. "Data? I'm not sure I –"

"You know," Jan continued. "Have you discovered how the good folks at the Lake Site Inn feel about this potential project?" She tilted her head and cast her eyes down the row to where Miles remained motionless, his face unreadable.

Her meaning now dawned on Sondra. "Ah, yes. The Lake Site. Well, it is the case we are aware certain private properties located in close proximity to the present site of Lake Kathleen may be impacted by its removal and restoration to a natural river basin."

Jan recognized in Miles's demeanor he wouldn't speak publicly here of his concerns. "Well," she snorted, wanting to come to his defense. "If I read between the lines, and bear in mind I'm only one of the rural locals here and not one of you academics," she swiveled her head slowly and raised her eyebrows in emphasis. This elicited several snickers. "I believe what you mean is that the Lake Site Inn is going to get the shaft, eh?"

"All I can say at this time is we are certainly aware of the potential for impact to local property owners, particularly those close to the Lake Kathleen basin."

"I'm sure that's comforting to the locals," deadpanned Jan, causing even more laughter.

Desperate to return to solid footing, Sondra readdressed the crowd. "If there are no other public comments, then I invite anyone who is interested in speaking with our group to meet with us privately after this gathering has dispersed."

Rick watched as she gave a perfunctory scan of the crowd before quickly moving to join her associates who stood nearly as one to vacate the assembly.

"Nice associate you have there Erasmus." Jan had somehow managed to navigate the departing crowd and took the empty seat next to him. "Gives a whole new meaning to what we used to call a stick in the mud." She jabbed him on the shoulder. "That's gotta be funny to you biology types."

"Peter's got a valid point, Jan," he said. "And, it's a little strange the DNR didn't object to the very same issue. Either they were unaware of the flower pollen in the final report, which I seriously doubt, or they were willing to overlook it in favor of the project."

"What are you saying?"

"I'm not sure, really. Something doesn't add up, but regardless, the issue's been made public now, so it will have to be –"

The large frame of Mike Pritchard suddenly loomed over the both of them. "Could have damn well used your support, Jan."

"Yeah, well Mike, I suppose you could have," she replied matter of factly. "Are you frustrated with me, because I decided to throw a bone to Miles instead of backing your little business? A business, I might add, which could just as well be accomplished with or without the damn dam. Or, is your anger really directed to the possibility that no one in this audience gives a flying fish how your particular business fares in this matter?"

Mike's face tensed as he attempted to control his anger. "I've spent the better part of ten years building my business and my client base," he said, raising his voice as he continued. "And I'll be damned if I won't be heard about what that bitch says is happening with the river basin!"

The uniformed police officer materialized next to Rick, startling him.

"Sir," she directed at Mike. "I'm going to have to ask you to lower your voice and watch your language."

Mike initially regarded her with contempt before allowing his face to relax. He glanced to Jan and found her staring fixedly at the floor, and then he turned to the man seated next to her. Unfortunately, Rick realized, he was wearing an old Biological Station sweatshirt. "You one of them?" Mike asked coolly.

"By them," Rick said, "I assume you mean from the Station?"

Mike merely nodded.

"Yes, I'm one of the research faculty here. I'm Rick Parsons." Rick reflexively extended a hand in greeting.

Mike ignored his gesture. "Do you support this project?"

Jan's head lifted, and she turned toward him. "Alright Mike, that's enough."

"No. It's ok, Jan," Rick said. He gave a tentative look to the officer, who continued to stare passively at the exchange, though he noticed she had subtly rested a hand on the butt of her sidearm. "Frankly, I could care less one way or another about the restoration. I think it's great when any ecosystem is returned to its natural state, but that always has to be balanced against the costs, and in this case, I think there are some viable concerns. Some were raised here, and others weren't."

"Are we done here, Mike?" Jan said evenly, her lips compressed in a thin line.

"Yeah, we're done here, alright," he replied, turning on his heel and making his way forcefully through the thinning crowd.

As Jan watched him leave, Rick turned to the officer. "May I ask why you are here in the first place?" He realized his tone was a little abrupt. "Sorry if that was rude. I guess I'm just curious."

The officer's utility belt made a leathery sound as she adjusted it. "No offense taken," she said. "Let's just say that someone wanted a police presence at this meeting, and that duty fell on me." Her eyes shifted to Jan. "You ok?"

Jan chuckled. "You mean Mike? That's no biggie. Well, at least he's not a problem for me." She saw a look of confusion on Rick's face. "Erasmus Parsons, meet Abigail Bennett." Before either could reply, she laughed again. "Let me amend. I've known you both so long I forgot we're supposed to be adults. Let's try again. Professor Erasmus Parsons, meet Officer Bennett of the Cheboygan Police Department." Jan sat back with a smile on her face, clearly pleased with herself at this awkward introduction.

Rick was first to try smooth things. "It's Rick," he said extending a hand. "Rick Parsons."

"Abigail Bennett," she replied politely then realizing her place in the situation added, "I guess here it's best to be Officer Bennett."

"Well, Officer Bennett," he said. "May I ask again who thought it was necessary to have you here this evening?"

"Not again," she replied, smiling almost mischievously.

"I'm sorry?"

"Before, you asked me *why* I was here. Now you just asked me *who* requested police presence. Those are two different questions."

"Don't flirt with the man, Abby," Jan goaded, her face again amused at creating another awkward moment. "Why don't you just answer his question?"

Abigail thought momentarily at giving her a rebuke but decided to let it pass, turning instead to Rick. "No flirtation, I assure you. As for your questions," she emphasized the plural, "all I am able answer at this point is that there was reason to believe that things might get acrimonious here this evening."

Rick was impressed with her choice of words but said nothing.

"And evidently," she added, "those concerns were valid."

Chapter 7

"I still need copies of your permit applications for my records."

Rick reminded himself it was too early in the term to pick a fight with Monica, who did her best to make everyone's life complicated at the station, befitting more a picky bureaucrat than what was really for the most part a laid back summer camp. For the moment, he ignored her, gesturing instead to one of the students who watched intently as they gathered supplies. "You'll find a half dozen or so of the collecting jars in the cabinet in the storage room. Make sure to get the 10 micron nets. There's a good chance they're still attached to the jars from last fall anyway." He turned to another. "Why don't you go with him and locate the large box marked 'Vernier'. It should be with the jars, and we'll need those too." The girl nodded wordlessly and fell in behind her classmate as they walked from the dock uphill toward the Aquatics Building.

"Did you hear me, Professor Parsons?" Monica called down.

Rick watched the pair move up the path toward the building, where Monica stood partway in the open rear access door looking particularly peeved at him. "Monica, I filed those electronically a few weeks ago, and I copied you on the submissions." He turned back to the four students who stood idly next to the pontoon boat and whispered. "Drives me crazy. That's the lab coordinator, and let me give you some advice. Don't make her angry at you. She's not going to shower you with warmth and fuzzies no matter how much you try to be nice, and she will give you a hard time if you don't take care of the equipment or put things away." He turned to her again. "You might check your spam folder, just in case. I used the Federal Application site to copy you, and your email server may have quarantined it."

He saw the questioning expressions on the students' faces. "We have to apply for collection permits for what we do in the field, even if it's as trivial as removing a few dozen vials of lake water for analysis. The lab coordinator," he gestured with his thumb in her direction, though she'd already closed the access door, "is responsible for keeping our applications on file, in case for some reason we're audited." The students nodded stoically. "And for the record, despite what she just said, I want to remind you that it's Rick and not Professor Parsons, ok? Applications and filings are formal enough here in the north woods, for goodness sakes. Don't misunderstand, I'm all for following the appropriate rules, but I have to draw the line at the 'Dr. Parsons' thing."

They all turned at the sound of gravel beneath the tires of a green pick up truck with the Alliance logo emblazoned on the passenger door. It pulled abruptly to a stop near the side entrance, trailing a small cloud of backlit dust that gathered around the wheels until it caught in the slight breeze from the lower road. Sondra stepped from the driver's side and began walking toward the building entrance, before she spotted the group assembled below. "Is that you Rick?" she called down, changing direction toward them.

"Yep. It's me. Good morning."

"Taking a class out this early?" she replied hurriedly as she reached them, nodding perfunctorily to the students who stood mutely.

"Most of you remember Sondra from her talk a few evenings ago?" Rick said to the students as a way of a loose introduction. "Sondra, these are the students who are taking my freshwater algae class on Mondays and Wednesdays."

She ignored this completely, instead putting both hands in the air in a display of exasperation. "Please tell me you aren't planning to use the temperature probes this morning."

Rick glanced over her shoulder at the approach of the two students who'd gone for supplies. "That depends which ones you mean." He gestured to the Vernier box, "Jenny's got the deep water probes we use for benthic measurements." He opened the cardboard lid and showed her the contents. "These are a little dated, but they still interface with the monitors." He dug around the box until he located two worn handheld devices. "Here they are." Rick attempted to power one on. "Deader than a doornail. Should've thought of that. Jenny, would you mind going back inside and asking Monica if we have two sets of double A batteries?" He glanced again to Sondra and read the impatience in her expression. "So, the answer is yes – we're going to use these this morning to do some base measurements for the depths where we collect."

"And when will you be back?"

"Look, Sondra. I know you want to start collecting temperatures on the river."

She nodded curtly, her lips compressed in a thin line.

"So why not take the remote probes Peter typically uses? They're a heck of lot easier to work. I believe you used them last fall."

"Yes," she blurted. "Of course I want those probes! It'd be nice to do some salinity and oxygenation co-measurement with the temperature."

Rick wasn't exactly sure where this was headed. "Well, there you go," and then it dawned on him. "Oh, let me guess. Peter's got them."

"No. His graduate student does. I ran into Peter this morning coming out of the dining hall and asked him about the probes, and he rather smugly told me she needed to use them for several days, which I find hard to believe."

Rick stole a quick glance to his assembled students, noticing their discomfort at the awkward exchange. "Sondra, I'm not sure what to tell you. I understand you may be frustrated with Peter, and to be candid I want to stay out of that situation." He nodded his head back toward the lake over his shoulder. "These students are new to collection methods, and we're planning on getting some samples from roughly a dozen sites. We'll only be gone a couple hours tops then back here so that I can get them started with learning how to classify." He eyed her meaningfully. "If you can wait, you're welcome to these old probes. At least you'll be able to get some data, but remember, you won't have remote capability."

Sondra checked her watch then looked absently toward the water. "I guess that will have to do. I'd initially planned to take data from the upper portions of the East Branch and then work my way down toward the Lake Kathleen. But I really want the probes Peter has for the upper stretch." Rick was nearly taken aback when she gave him a resigned smile. "Thanks all the same. I'll take you up on your suggestion. I'll just switch my plan and do Kathleen first. Your probes will be fine for that part."

With that, she nodded politely to the students and turned toward the car.

#

Rick cut the engine and let the pontoon boat drift idly toward the near shore. He motioned to the approaching narrow strip of sandy beach. "The boat will run aground here any moment, and we can jump out in the shallows." The students looked dubiously over the side, seeing only dark shades of blue where the water was still quite deep, and Rick laughed. "Don't worry. I'm not going to make you jump in right here!" This brought a few smiles. "The drop off is steep where the point hooks around." He gestured to a spot in the water twenty feet in front of the bow where the lake abruptly changed color to varied shades of yellow. "I think it goes from almost fifty feet deep to about a foot and a half in the space of only a dozen yards." At this, the bow passed leisurely into the shallows, and the bottom revealed itself as rippled sand, interspersed with water sedge and small shells drifting back and forth.

"This place is called Hook Point," Rick said, pointing to one of the students to throw the anchor and line out toward shore. "You can just toss that out." As she obeyed, they heard the distinctive rasp of the aluminum pontoon cutting into the soft sand. "It's usually sheltered here from the waves, so don't worry too much with the anchor. It's mostly to keep the boat from drifting once we all get off."

The six students then waited dutifully on the bench chairs in the bow, and Rick took the opportunity for some formalities. "Ok then," he began. "Here's my big spiel. You all are new to the Bug Camp, and so I'm happy to have the honor of teaching your first course. Most of what you'll do will involve learning by immersion, beginning with this morning. By the end of the term, you will have gained experience in exploring algal communities from various habitats, including differing locations within Douglas Lake, a few surrounding river ecosystems, a couple of bog sites, and even from spots in the Great Lakes. I want you to become skilled in various techniques for collecting and preserving algae. You will then learn to identify a range of algal species using both traditional microscopy and the scanning electron microscope."

"Hopefully you remember, algae are single-celled photosynthetic producers. They capture radiant energy from the sun and convert it, along with carbon dioxide, into simple and complex sugars they use for metabolism. As such, they form a critical base of the trophic pyramid, providing essential biomass for higher organisms while at the same time serving a key role in nutrient cycling." Rick swept his hand down the shore to the left. "Take a look at Sedge Point over there. It's begins where you can see those cedars leaning way over the water. See them?" He then moved his arm across his body until his hand came to rest in the direction of Hook Point to the right. "I want you to look at the type of producers you see here along this stretch of shoreline. What do you notice?"

"Mostly pines?" exclaimed a student hesitantly.

"That's right," said Rick. "In fact, along this shore you are likely to find mostly cedar and white pine, with an occasional poplar or birch thrown in where the canopy has thinned from some disturbance. And here," he added, casting his eyes about the water, "there are a few water sedges. Oh, of course there are other trees and plants in the understory, but mostly this place allows these three types of producers to thrive." Then he pointed across the open water to where Grapevine Point thrust outward. "Now, if you go for a hike around Grapevine Point –" He stopped midsentence. "As a side bar, make sure you all go walk the trails of Grapevine. You can access them from the gate next to the Aquatics Building. It's beautiful there.

Every year students put up hammocks between trees on the upslope of Grapevine just to enjoy the peace and quiet."

"Anyway, when you go to Grapevine, take a look around at the trees. Most are deciduous, even right down to the water's edge. You'll find aspen and birch, silver and sugar maple, and stands of beech. What's my point? My point is that where a specific tree thrives is linked in part to its habitat, which includes the right alchemy of abiotic factors like sunlight, nutrients, water and such, and the influences of competition and predation. In this field class, you'll come to find that producers like algae exhibit the same phenomenon. Some grow in certain places and among certain specific cohabitants, and others grow elsewhere. You'll learn to distinguish various biotic and abiotic factors that affect where algae species live, and you will learn about the influence of climactic and environmental change on this fundamental group of producers."

Rick motioned toward the boxes with the probes and the sampling jars. "Enough of my formal and dare I say motivating introduction!" Then in a lower voice he added, "How was it?"

The same red-headed girl who threw out the anchor scooped up the temperature probe box and used her foot to slide the one with the sampling jars to the student seated next to her. "Well, I'm motivated to go collect some pond scum!"

Rick laughed. "I don't suppose you know someone named Jan, do you?"

She shook her head.

"No? Well, I have to admit that's a fitting coincidence." He then jumped carefully from the boat's side platform into the calf deep water and began walking toward the narrow beach. "Sometime you all ought to go have breakfast at the Brutus Camp Deli. It's south of Pellston about six miles or so. Chances are you'll get waited on by an old friend of mine. Name's Jan." He waited for the others to join him on the beach. "We sort of grew up here, and she likes to make fun of what I became. Calls me a pond scum scientist."

They began walking around the shore, having to step carefully to avoid hundreds of tiny baby toads that must have recently emerged from the boggy woods beyond. "Is it true the lake hasn't changed much in decades?" asked a dark-haired young man.

"Yes and no," Rick replied. "One of things I love about it here is that it's difficult to see much change on a large scale." He stopped and turned to face them. "If you look out here around the lake, all you can see if virgin forest. It's amazing really. The station has protected so much of the shoreline and surrounding woods." He cast his eyes about the horizon. "From here, it looks identical to what it was like when I was a child, and that's pretty special."

"What about on the west side of the lake?"

"Well, there are cottages there, and most are getting pretty old. Some bigger homes have come in, but they've been built back from the waterfront and out of view. People used to come here only in the summer, but now there are several who live here year round. So, yeah, there have been changes." He glanced across North Fishtail toward East Point. "Over there, there used to be a natural pool set back a few feet from the shore behind the tall grasses along the ridge. It was really a small bog. I remember when I was young, we'd go there to see the pollywogs swimming in the tannin colored water, and we'd sometimes interrupt a student from the Bug Camp doing some sort of measurement. That was over forty years ago, and now the bog's long gone." He laughed again and looked at them. "The students are still here."

"What about the lake itself?" asked the red-haired girl.

"Same thing," said Rick. From a distance, it looks about the same as it always did, apart from being higher or lower depending on the winter snows and the amount of rain. But, when you take a closer look, you'll find major changes."

"Like?"

"Well, I can speak to the algae of course!" he said smiling. "Seriously, it was only a few years ago that zebra mussels exploded in this lake, and they decimated the producer populations. The lake became even clearer than what it is today, if you can believe that. Many of the benthic algae were overgrazed, and the population dynamics were drastically affected." He took the box of collecting jars from the young boy who carried it and placed it on the sand, opened the lid, and reached in to withdraw a small vial with a collecting net attached. "But things change. The zebras are falling, the algae are returning. The macrophyte population is reorganizing itself. It's all interconnected." He lifted the vial and showed it to them. "Let me show you how to use this thing. We'll do some sampling along the shoreline here and also at a point around the hook where the bottom gets a little silted with organic matter." He nodded to the red-haired girl. "Bring along those temp probes. We'll do our first round of collecting here, then go sample a few more deep water locations. After that, we'll head back to the lab, and I'll show you how to prep the samples for identification. This will take a few days of microscope work, because you're just getting started, but you'll get pretty good at coding in no time."

Chapter 8

The trees along Grapevine cast long shadows far across the bay, and while the tops of the tallest trees on the near shore still reflected a touch of golden light, the sunset wasn't long to arrive. Rick sat idly in an old Adirondack chair on the back porch, slowly savoring the remaining sips of beer from a bottle he'd been nursing for over a half hour. The wind had died with the close of the day, leaving the water uncharacteristically smooth as glass, save for the places here and there where some fish softly broke the surface and created rings of tiny waves that moved outward. From somewhere high overhead, he heard a "whoosh whoosh" of a large bird as it arced across the upper boughs of the shoreline trees and vanished in a stand of woods on the far side.

The rasp of an old screen door spring sounded so near in the stillness of the oncoming twilight that he glanced quickly to the cottage next door. There was no sign of Heather, not even a light left on in anticipation of her return, though his eyes caught movement down the shore as two figures, probably students, emerged from their tiny tin-roofed shack and walked slowly up the main road toward what was likely an impromptu party outside the upper road cabins. He laughed softly, wondering if Heather had decided to join them in one of the several, what did they call them? The circles? He laughed again, envisioning her stretched out within a hammock between two trees, one of a coterie of partying students celebrating summer in camp style. He couldn't exactly imagine her drinking cheap beer and chilling to whatever music was the flavor of the season. It used to be the Grateful Dead many years ago, but now ... these students weren't even born when the Dead was on its last gasp.

He took another look down the row of faculty cabins, mostly out of procrastination. There weren't many signs of activity at all. Everyone, it seemed, had something better to do, or at least had something that needed doing. "Alright then," he said aloud, draining the remainder of his beer and checking his watch. He debated going inside to get another bottle and returning to the comfort of the porch, waiting for someone or something came along. Instead, he walked into the kitchen and grabbed his daypack, slung it over his shoulder, and left through the front door.

He turned right on the gravel road toward the main camp and had taken only a few steps when he heard muffled laughter of several people coming toward him from the direction of the old fire road behind. Three students emerged from the two track that led up through the fishtail woods. They laughed and spoke openly, completely unaware of his presence.

"Back from a little walk?" he said in a matter of fact tone.

The trio abruptly stopped, and the young woman gave a stifled yelp.

"Jesus!" cried out one of the boys.

Rick was thankful it had become too dark for them to see his suppressed smile. "Sorry! I didn't know how else to warn you I was standing here."

"Professor Parsons?" said the other boy in a voice that sounded hopeful.

"Gets a little dark in those woods about now, doesn't it?"

The three glanced to one another, not sure if they were being reprimanded for doing something there weren't supposed to be doing. The girl let her words tumble quickly. "We didn't know there was anything wrong with going for a night walk."

Rick's voice softened, and he stepped closer so they could see his face more easily. "Relax. There's no rule against anything like that." He then recognized the boy who spoke first. "Is that you Zack?"

"Yes, Professor."

"You mean, Rick?" He laughed then, softly. "Remember we're up north here, and I'd prefer a little less formal, ok?" He saw their faces relax. "How far up did you all go? All the way to North Fishtail?"

"Only about half way," said the girl.

Rick nodded. "Let me guess. You found the little trail off the two track that leads to the beach midway between the bays."

"We wanted to see the sunset," said Zack. "And we stuck around for a while until it got darker before heading back."

"Any bears?" Rick added playfully.

The other boy's eyes widened slightly. "You're kidding, right? Bears?"

Rick laughed again. "Actually, there are bears here, though you're not likely to see them. You keep hiking at night like this, however, and you'll most certainly come across either raccoons or skunks."

"We thought it was ok to go after dark."

"Ok?" said Rick. "Of course it's ok. In fact, I encourage you to do that. I can't tell you how many times I've hiked in the woods around the point after dark. Bring a flashlight, and every once in a while shine it off the path into the deep woods. You'll be surprised how many sets of eyes reflect back at you!" He nodded toward the main camp. "I'm heading in."

"Into camp?" said Zack.

Rick patted his backpack. "Back to the lab. I figured I might as well get some focused time for my own work."

The four began walking up the road toward the administration buildings. "More algae?" said Zack.

Rick chuckled. "Yep, more algae." He gave a soft hello as they passed by two students who lounged in faded hammocks near the first of the row of old tin cabins by the shore. "More specifically, it's diatoms."

"Like the ones we identified earlier today?"

"That's right. Part of my own work examines how diatom species change over time. I've been sampling certain places here around both Douglas and Burt Lakes for several years."

"Is that why you stopped to do a sample in the middle of the bay on our way back this afternoon?"

Rick nodded. "That's why. Well, I also wanted your group to see the technique for collecting a deep water sample and doing the baseline measurements. That place we stopped is almost seventy feet, and it's rather silted down in the lower benthic region. After the lake turns in the spring and settles into its summer mode, there's a period where the diatoms, particularly the non-colony ones, fall toward the bottom."

"What class are you two talking about?" asked the girl.

"Freshwater Algae," replied Rick. "Are you doing two terms this summer?"

"Yes."

"Good. Well, then if you're not already scheduled for the second term, and you have an interest in learning about algae, it would be great to have you in the field with us."

She turned to Zack. "I thought you were doing invertebrates or something like that."

Zack saw the perplexed expression on Rick's face. "I was telling her about collecting from the snails."

"Got it," Rick said, turning to her again. "I had the students collect a few snails from the silt near the transition zone around big shoal. They're called *Elimia livescens*, and they're pretty common around the lakes here. They're also a fairly good host for some algae species."

"Algae on snails," she said dubiously.

"They do," replied Rick. "In fact, there's a big difference in the type of diatoms which attach to the snails between Douglas Lake and Burt Lake, which is a curious indicator of the difference between their water environments."

"And that's what you're doing now?" said Zack. "You're examining the samples?"

"I am," said Rick. "I'm going to the lab to do essentially what your class did earlier today. I want to see if some old friends have turned up in the usual places."

"Old friends," the girl quipped. "Seriously?"

Rick laughed. "Ok, that's a bit nerdy I'll admit. But, I am curious to see if there have been any changes in this particular location. We've been keeping records on many sites for over thirty years now, and it's interesting to see how the colonization patterns look, particularly with the influence of global warming."

They passed by an old cinder block building where the station library was housed, and Zack gestured to a worn trail which led uphill from the main road toward the secondary row of student cabins midway up the slope. "You sure you wouldn't rather join us?"

"It's tempting," said Rick. "I appreciate the offer. How about I take a rain check."

"Sounds good, Professor Parsons," said the girl, then seeing his slightly pained expression she amended quickly, "I mean, err, Rick."

"Hey, that's better," he replied. "And guys," he paused to get their full attention. "Watch out for bears."

#

The refrigerator compressor suddenly shut down, and the lab became quiet, save for the soft noise of the wind blowing through the open window. Rick glanced up from where he was seated and peered outside to the dark bay below. The water spread out in shades of indigo, broken by the reflection of the moon against the wavy surface, while the shoreline of trees on either side rose upward as a dark barrier. His brief reverie was interrupted by the bobbing motion of a flashlight beam from someone returning home along the Grapevine Point trail. The light blinked in and out between the trunks along the water's edge.

He returned his attention to the gooseneck lamp next to the microscope and used his hand to dim the light until the room itself was barely illuminated. He turned on the stage bulb and was about to position one of the slides he'd prepared earlier when there came a shuffling noise outside the hallway.

"Is there someone here?" Heather called tentatively toward the open lab door from the hall.

Rick set the slide down gently on the table and turned his head toward the door. "It's just me."

She pushed the door open enough to poke her head into the lab, glancing first to the dark bank of overhead bulbs before finding him across the room within the circle of his private light. "Is that you, Rick?"

"Yep."

She looked about the room and took a hesitant step inside. "Why are you in the dark?"

He laughed softly. "It's ok. C'mon in. I'm about to have a quick look at my samples to see what turns up."

"In the dark."

"It's not that dark!" He motioned for her to come join him at the bench. "Ok. Maybe it's a little dark, but your eyes will adjust. I like this better than the harsh lights."

She pulled an adjacent stool from underneath the bench and took a seat next to him. Rick eyed her accusingly. "What?"

"So how was the Lake Site?" he said simply, enjoying the slight expression of surprise on her face.

"How did you –"

"No offense, but you smell like fried chicken. It's a give away."

Her lips formed a slight pout in mock hurt, and then she laughed and turned up her hands in a gesture of admission. "Peg and I went for a late dinner, and we just got back a half hour ago."

"You here to do some work too?"

Heather lifted her arm and sniffed the fabric of her blouse. "I don't smell like chicken."

He laughed again. "Believe me, I could sense Lake Site on you the moment you entered the room." She gestured to a door on the far side of the room that led to a connecting hallway for another lab. "The answer is no. I'm not doing anything that important. I just came to make sure Monica prepped all the supplies for my morning class tomorrow."

"So how was dinner?"

"Well, dinner itself was fine. It was afterward that

things got interesting."

"I'm all ears."

"After dinner, Peg and I decided to have a glass of wine at the bar."

"I assume Stuart was there."

"Of course he was there. He recognized us. Well, at least he knew Peg."

Rick chuckled. "Everybody within fifty miles knows Peg."

"At any rate," she continued. "It was getting late, and we had the bar to ourselves." Heather leaned in slightly and gave him a meaningful look. "While he was cleaning up, he chatted with us about the dam removal."

"Go on."

Heather shook her head. "Apparently the owner is fairly upset about the project."

"You mean Miles?"

"Yes, that's his name. I forgot you worked there once."

"Years ago when I was in my late teens. A couple of summers waiting tables. I was there when Miles took over the place."

"Well, according to Stuart, he's hired a lawyer to try to overturn the project."

"I don't think there's much he can do," said Rick. "I think the Lake Site sold the property years ago, except for the small wedge up from the shore where the restaurant sits. Any interest they had in maintaining the lake was transferred to the new owner, whom I know was perfectly willing to work with Alliance."

"From what Stuart hinted, the owner is deeply concerned about the lake being drained."

Rick nodded. "I bet he is. People come for the view as much as the chicken." Rick's mouth formed a smirk. "I can still smell it on you, by the way."

Heather's eyes widened. "Are you serious?"

His lips parted in a sheepish grin. "Don't worry, I'm sure some people find it attractive."

For a moment, she considered making a sarcastic reply. "Evidently, the owner doesn't think much of Sondra."

"Stuart told you this?"

"He's overheard some choice words. Said Miles was fuming after returning to the Inn from the project update last week."

Rick shrugged his shoulders and lifted a hand slightly. "As I said, I don't think there's much he can do, legally or otherwise."

"I think it's the *otherwise* that is the real concern."

"I seriously doubt Miles would do anything – "

The sound of a door opening from somewhere down the hall caught their attention, and the pair waited as footfalls approached on the linoleum.

"Is there someone in the lab?" came the distinctive voice of Peter Cunningham.

Rick rolled his eyes at Heather.

"We're in here, Peter," she called softly. She held his gaze a few moments, both reluctant to give up the privacy of the setting.

Peter pushed open the lab door and hastily reached for the switch. Instantly, the room transformed into something harsh and cold, the bright lights casting everything in sharp relief. "What in God's name are you two doing in here?"

Rick glanced once again to the large window, disappointed to find the bay had been replaced by the mirror reflection of the lab's interior. He reached for the gooseneck and shut off the light then turned to Peter as he approached from the doorway. "Hello, Peter." Rick stifled a laugh when he saw the perplexed expression on his colleague's face. "You caught us, Peter," he baited. "We snuck away from camp past curfew to have our own private party."

Peter regarded them both with mild disdain. "It's really none of my business what you two have conspired. I only came in to download the collection data onto my computer and happened to overhear your discussion from the hallway."

For a moment, Heather considered amending Rick's statement, but she remained silent, deciding instead to enjoy the small fantasy.

"You've been on the river?"

Peter glanced to the microscope and the collection of mounts on the table nearby, dawning on him that he was the butt of another joke. "I have," he said coldly. "I've spent the better part of several hours doing gradient measurements along the transect in my primary location."

"Are you *both* working in that area?" Heather added.

If the question bothered Peter, Rick couldn't sense any change in his emotion. "No," he said curtly. "Elise has been working up the West Branch for the past two days trying to locate another site."

"Ah," replied Rick. "And how goes it with your latest find?"

Peter looked cautiously from one to the other. "That depends where you stand."

"Where we stand?" echoed Heather, her face registering confusion. "What are you suggesting?"

Peter faced Rick directly. "I understand you were rather noncommittal the other evening."

Rick took a deep breath and turned toward Heather. "Remember that guy in the audience the other night who was a little confrontational with Sondra?"

"You mean the guy asking about predatory fish."

"That's him. His name is Mike Pritchard. He runs a private fly fishing guide service on the Maple. After Sondra finished, he came over to where we were seated and got a little testy with a friend of mine."

"The woman who runs the Camp Deli?"

"Yeah, though Jan can take care of herself just fine. This guy Pritchard wanted to know my position on the project, and I told him the truth, which he didn't like. I really just wanted to keep out of it." Rick met Peter's gaze. "And I don't remember saying anything that could be construed as supporting one side or the other, Peter."

Peter was about to reply when Rick cut him short. "And from what you said the other night, I have to admit I was a little surprised that you have such a protective interest in the sport fishing along the river."

Heather laughed softly at this, which caused Peter to flinch. "I could give a damn about that, Erasmus. My interest foremost concerns my research and the potential detriment to the east basin once the dam is removed."

"Many would argue that restoring the natural flow is a good thing," Rick countered.

"And I claim there's too much risk to the protective species."

"And of course your funding too, isn't that right?" Rick said. The look on Peter's face confirmed he had overstepped the mark. Before he could reply, Rick amended, "Peter, I said I am neutral on this whole thing, and that's the truth. You can decide whether or not to believe or trust either Heather or me. In the meantime, I am interested in what you've found with the new site. Has it flowered?"

Peter remained silent for several seconds before nodding slowly. "You know my primary site?"

Rick shook his head yes.

"Just a dozen yards downstream on the east side,

there's a soft embankment where a few white cedars form a group. The plant forbe grows near the base, set back a little from the water close to where the old deer trail cuts south. There are tubular flowers now. Brilliant yellow with the spotted lip."

"And?"

Peter smiled slightly, which was the first time Heather had ever seen him do so. "When I passed the area on my way back from collecting data, I noticed a few bees near the blossoms."

"Was there anything to sample?"

Peter shook his head. "I'm going back tomorrow in the early afternoon, once the air warms enough."

"Monkeyflower opens in the afternoon?" said Heather.

"The flowers below the dam release in midday, when they do at all. If anything comes from this new site, my guess is it will be at a similar time."

"If at all," Rick added.

Peter nodded soberly. "If at all."

"And if you do get pollen, will be enough to overturn the project?" said Heather.

"It damn well ought to!" Peter demanded. "Between the Hungerford Beetle scarcity and this new Monkeyflower site, the DNR simply can't turn the other cheek to the possible hydrologic risks."

"Which reminds me," Rick interjected. "I ran into Sondra this morning before my class. She was looking for the good temperature probes and thought I might be using them on the lake."

Peter's face cooled visibly.

"I told her you had them," Rick said.

"Elise needs them on the West Branch."

"Ahh," Rick replied, not wanting to push the issue further. "I didn't realize she was doing data collection." He glanced furtively to Heather and saw a flicker of disbelief in her eyes. "I told her she could have the older probes my class used today once we were finished." He suddenly stood up and walked across the room and through a doorway to a connecting hall, calling back to them after a few seconds. "Yeah, the probes are gone from the storage bin." Rick reentered the lab and rejoined them. "She must have taken them this afternoon."

Peter pursed his lips and stared absently at a point on the floor. In a soft voice he asked, "Did she say where she was planning to start measuring?"

"Not exactly," said Rick. "Probably along various points up toward your site, beginning at Lake Kathleen."

Peter looked up from the floor and gave a curt nod to them both then said in the same soft voice, "Very well." And without another word, he spun around and walked out the lab door and into the hall.

Chapter 9

Sunshine flooded the cleared acre of flat ground above camp, where midsummer wildflowers flourished among the tall grasses, dotting the landscape with splashes of white campion and oxeye daisies, purple knapweeds and yellow Rudbeckia. Heat waves shimmered off sandy ground, mixing with the humid air above and making the field appear almost dreamy from where David stood to wipe the sweat off his brow.

"I'll go check the last one," said the young woman several yards away, pointing loosely to what looked like a small greenhouse made from PVC pipe.

"Be my guest," he said smiling. "Hope it's hot enough for you!"

Susan glanced quickly overhead. "There's not a cloud in sky at all." She began to walk over toward the research pod, calling back to him over her shoulder, "I thought you said it was normally cool up north during the summer? I'm baking out here!"

"It's always hotter up here on the hill," he replied. "We're protected from the wind off the lake, and the sand reflects the sun." He watched as she neared the flow box attached to the greenhouse wall. "You think it's bad now, wait until next month!"

Susan first peered inside the plastic sheeting. "These look fine." She walked slowly around the square base then bent down closely on the far side. "A couple of

Sulphurs have emerged!" A pair of pale yellow butterflies flitted among the plants inside.

David waved to signal he'd heard her and gave her a thumb's up. "What's the level on that one?"

She followed the ventilating duct from the greenhouse base to a regulating box a few feet away. "The CO_2 is within range, and the flow is good. Do you want me to do anything?"

He let his eyes scan the remaining greenhouses spaced throughout the open field before answering her. "Naw, it's ok. We'll give them another day or so of elevation, before we start the next round of tissue measurement."

He was about to say something else, when he caught sight of Rick approaching from the lower trail, emerging from a shaded stand of cedar into the bright sunshine of the open field. "God it's hot up here!" Rick stated flatly.

"Well, hello there Professor Parsons," David said kindly, reaching out with a sweaty palm to shake Rick's as he approached. "What brings you up this way?"

Rick's eyes squinted as he adjusted from the relative darkness of the camp trail. He put a hand over his forehead and looked out toward Susan, who waved at him in greeting. "Is that Susan? I can hardly see out here, it's so bright."

"Quit complaining," David joked. "He jerked a thumb in her direction. "She's perfectly happy to do the grunt work out here, and I'm perfectly happy to let her."

Rick smiled slyly and shook his head in mock disgust. "Ahh, what it must be like to have your own doctoral student. Or should I say personal gopher."

"Susan's actually a terrific student, and she has a good sense of humor. She might even find you funny."

"Is it just the two of you doing this, or do you let

your ecology class share some of the work?"

David chuckled and wiped his forehead again. "Oh, I'll bring them up here in a few days once we start the tissue measurements. I have to make sure they're competent with the spectrometer and the chromatograph first, before I let them have at it with my data."

Rick moved a few paces to the nearest greenhouse and peered inside the plastic sheeting, where a half dozen pots each contained a single deep green plant. "Peas?" Rick said, in a voice something between a statement and a question. At that moment, a butterfly flitted from the underside a leaf and landed on one of the other plants. "That's a Sulphur?"

"Cloudless Sulphur," replied David, who joined him and now bent down to point at one of the plants near the greenhouse edge. "Take a look there."

It took a moment for Rick to see the nearly camouflaged caterpillar resting along one of the primary stems. Its lime green body was peppered with small black dots, and a thin yellow band extended from one end to the other.

"This is all that's in here?" he said.

David chuckled slightly. "As much as we can control." He gestured to the bottom of the greenhouse. "See how the pots rest on that base? The base is raised above the ground, and the plastic sheeting seals in the air as best we can." He anticipated Rick's follow up question. "And, you can see the access seam on the other side in the greenhouse wall."

Rick's eyes went from the pots to the seam and then to the connecting hose which attached to the bottom corner of the plastic wall. "This is where you circulate?"

David stood up and placed his hand proudly on a small regulating box a couple feet away, where a white flexible hose snaked outward and toward the wall. "My flow design." He pointed to a small wire with a probe near the top corner of the greenhouse frame. "The regulator monitors the carbon dioxide levels in the enclosure and adjusts it to our test parameters."

Again, Rick surveyed the field. "How many of these things are you running?"

"There are twenty two in the upper plot here, and I have another dozen in the small clearing where the old tower used to be. Some of the houses serve as atmospheric controls, while the others we keep at elevated carbon dioxide levels."

"That's a helluva set up." He glanced over across the field to where Susan was bent over peering into another greenhouse. "And just the two of you manage this?"

David used the back of his hand to wipe his forehead. "The short answer is no. Susan's funded by the NSF grant, and the two of us are able to handle things for the first couple of weeks while the caterpillars start feeding. Like I said, once the term gets underway, I'll bring the ecology class up here right away to show them what an example of field research looks like. I can usually count on a few students to dovetail their own masters project with my work here." He eyed Rick somewhat mischievously. "And that way I get a few extra hands."

"How long is the grant funded?"

"One more summer after this one. We were able to apply for an extension based on last year's preliminary results, so I guess we'll be rolling in the dough for a little longer."

Rick smiled and repeated softly, "Rolling in the dough. I like that." He mused how the "well-funded" faculty here lived in such rustic housing in the confines of what was essentially a science summer camp. "And any surprises?"

"It's more interesting than surprising. We've been growing these plants for several weeks now in elevated carbon dioxide, and the caterpillars have been feasting and growing themselves. And some," he pointed to a flitting butterfly in a nearby enclosure, "have obviously begun to change. Susan and I did a preliminary round of plant tissue analysis, looking at carbon to nitrogen ratios."

"And?"

"It's what we predicted. The plants in the CO_2 grow more quickly and have a higher tissue density than those in the control, which is what you'd expect. However, the carbon to nitrogen ratios for the high CO_2 plants are statistically different. The test plants have less nitrogen per microgram of tissue. They are literally growing bigger while at the same time less – "

"Filling," Rick mused, clearly enjoying his colleague's enthusiasm.

David laughed, aware how he was getting carried away. "In a manner of speaking, you could put it that way. Bigger and less filling."

"Like a Twinkie," Rick offered.

"Like a Twinkie," he repeated, smiling as he said it. "I like that too, but I doubt the NSF will go for it in my next report."

Rick glanced again at the caterpillar inside. "What about these?"

"We haven't done the measurements on the herbivores yet this year. However, if things track like last summer, we should see a correlation in mass."

"Bigger?"

"Yes," David replied. "On the test plants, the elevated carbon dioxide resulted in pea plants that became larger but were less nutrient dense. The caterpillars on those plants also had more mass, mostly we think, because they had to eat more plant tissue to get the normal quantity of nutrients, like the nitrogen."

"And this ultimately means?" Rick asked.

David motioned for them to walk over to the field edge beneath the lower boughs of a shading cedar tree. "We're still working on that," he finally answered. "There are some important hypotheses for climate change, at least based on this local system. The plants become Twinkies, as you put it, and the herbivores have to gorge themselves in the process."

Rick thought about the vast majority of Americans who tended to eat the same way. "Sounds like nature's going to imitate what humans have been doing for a few decades."

"Yeah, it does," David chuckled. "Nutrient poor and gaining mass."

They both turned their heads at the sound of a fast approaching white truck on the far side of the field. It bounced along the two track on the perimeter of the border woods, angling for a hundred yards in their direction until the road veered off quickly downhill toward the main camp. David pursed his lips and made a soft whistle as he inhaled.

Rick winced. "That was Monica driving." He immediately did a quick mental inventory of all the supplies his class had used the past few days, wondering how many she likely considered 'overdue'.

David looked again across the field to the point where she'd emerged from the woods. "Don't see her up here much."

Rick nodded. "I guess not. Mostly, she's down in the labs doing preps and clean ups."

"Did you see that expression on her face?"

Rick's own was still frozen in what looked like someone afraid of having done something wrong. "Yeah, I saw it. Is there anybody doing work in the Grapevine Point woods?"

"I haven't seen anyone go out that way, though Susan and I have only been here for awhile. Tanner's class was in the computer lab this morning."

Tanner Evans was an ornithologist who specialized in eagle population dynamics, and he taught a field class in forest ecology. Rick particularly admired his humble personality and the ease at which he established rapport with his students.

"What about his grad student?" said Rick, remembering the small observatory shack in the middle of the woods set back from the point. He'd only met Tanner's doctoral student once at the opening ceremony a couple weeks ago, and she struck him as either introverted or painfully shy.

David merely shrugged. "Could be, though I can't imagine Monica tearing out of the woods because of her." His face formed a bemused expression. "Maybe she ran into Peter? That's how I react whenever I see him." He then regretted the comment and began to apologize. "Look, Rick. Forget that. Not exactly collegial on my part."

Rick turned once again toward the direction of the administration buildings, hearing in the distance the sound of sliding gravel as the station truck pulled quickly into the small gravel lot next door. "Don't worry about it, Dave. I think it's safe to say we've all had our unique experiences with Peter." He faced his friend again. "Actually, he's the reason I came up here to talk to you."

"Peter?"

"Well, not just Peter, though he's a part of my concern."

"Let me guess. Something to do with the Alliance relationship."

Rick gave him a wry smile. "That's a delicate way of putting it, yes." He became distracted as a large dragonfly buzzed between them and landed softly on a nearby stalk of Timothy grass. "What do you know about Peter's research?"

"I know he's pretty high profile." He saw Rick's eyebrows raise slightly. "Peter's been consulted by a few Federal committees on climate change and endangered plant species. I think he was even tapped several years ago when Gore was doing background work on the Inconvenient Truth film. You ever seen his vitae?"

Rick shook his head.

"I took a glance at his homepage not too long ago. He's done some impressive publications as a result of his work here at the camp."

The dragonfly suddenly lifted off and hovered for several seconds above the grass head, flew outward in a small circle around the nearest greenhouse, then returned to settle gently on Rick's shoulder.

"These things never cease to amaze me," Rick said, turning his head to study the dragonfly only inches away from his face. It remained motionless for a few seconds, until some flying insect out in the field caught its attention, and it bolted away in pursuit. Rick's eyes followed it across the open land until it became lost in the hazy glare. "We ran into Peter a couple evenings ago in the lab. We made the mistake of –"

"We?" David interrupted.

"Heather and I."

There was the slightest suggestion of a smirk on David's face. "Got it. You two continuing to work on something?"

Rick regarded his friend neutrally. In many ways, despite its deserved reputation as an institute of scientific field research and teaching, the Biological Station was indeed like a summer camp, where gossip and innuendo formed the bedrock of entertainment. When David failed to reply, Rick sighed. "We're just friends, and yes, there may have been something last year, but no, nothing ever came of it." He eyed him again appraisingly. "May I continue?"

To his credit, the smirk vanished. "You were saying about the other night?"

"Right. Couple nights ago. Peter interrupted us while we were in the main lab. He started rehashing his concerns about the dam proposal."

"Do you mean his concerns with Alliance, or his concerns with Sondra?" David quipped.

"That's the thing. He started badgering me about why I didn't jump to his defense that night. Then things took a slightly different tone. I know it's fairly obvious that he and Sondra don't exactly see eye to eye on the project."

"That's putting it mildly."

"Exactly my point," said Rick. "There was an undercurrent of threat in what he was saying to us."

"He threatened Sondra?"

"No. Not directly." Rick glanced down to his pants pocket, feeling his cell phone vibrate. "Peter's well aware that Sondra intended to collect her supplemental data the past few days up on the branch, and the way Peter spoke that night made both Heather and me uneasy, almost like he had something planned."

"I'm not exactly sure what he could do," said David. "I mean, the guy's a tenured Professor doing field research like the rest of us. You make it seem like there's something sinister – "

"Well that's the thing," Rick interrupted. "You said so yourself he's pretty committed to this location."

"Committed, yes. To the point of doing something drastic? I don't know about that."

Rick cell phone vibrated again, followed by a short musical tone signaling he'd received a voice message. He reached into his pocket and removed the device, taking a quick glance at the lit screen. "That's weird," he muttered.

"Let me guess, it's a call from Peter, wanting to tell you that he's sorry he scared you that night."

Rick unlocked his phone, pushed the playback button, and held the device to his ear. "It's from Peg," he said absently. "Something about Monica finding a station truck off the Branch." He remained silent for several moments then finally disconnected the cell and met his colleague's eyes.

"A truck?" said David. "Which truck? The one we just saw her whizzing by in?"

"I'm not sure. Peg just said it was the field truck Sondra used a couple days ago. Do you have your phone?"

David gave him a confused expression. "No. Don't carry it up here."

"Well, you're going to get a similar message from Peg. She said Charles is having her call all the faculty in for an emergency meeting."

David tried to imagine what could possibly cause the station director to do anything on short notice, particularly something characterized as an emergency. "What about students?" he asked, looking across the field to where Susan stood near one of the far greenhouse units.

"The message said just faculty and staff. Nothing about students."

"Dear God," whispered David, turning to face his friend again. "Did she say where?"

Rick nodded. "Main hall. We're supposed to be there at the top of the hour."

David glanced at his watch. "Alright. I'll be along shortly. Let me go tell Susan I've got an unscheduled meeting, and I'll meet you there."

#

The administration building was set back from the shore road, separated by a large cement area that served as a volleyball court and as a social space for various student and staff outdoor functions. Worn cement stairs on either side led to a covered walkway which ran along the building's length, where roughly a half dozen screen doors led into various staff and maintenance rooms. Peg stood outside the door in front of the mailroom, waiting for Rick as he approached from the far end. She gestured with one hand vaguely in the direction he'd come.

"I saw you come down the trail from the library."

Rick noticed her expression lacked the usual playfulness. "Yeah, I was up there talking with David."

"I just tried giving him – "

"He doesn't have a cell with him," Rick anticipated, taking his own from his pocket and waving it loosely for her to see. "I got your message and passed it along to him." Rick glanced over her shoulder to the far end, where another set of stairs rose to a small elevated gravel lot. He could just make out the front quarter of a black and white police cruiser parked next to what looked like the truck Monica drove shortly before. "He said he'll be along soon. What's going on, Peg?"

"I'm not sure," she replied, lowering her voice slightly as one of the students emerged from a door nearby that led into the station's general store. The two made eye contact, obligating Peg to say something in greeting. "Hey there, Julia. How's your summer so far?"

The girl smiled as she shouldered a worn backpack and emptied onto the walkway, stopping short when she caught sight of Rick standing nearby. "Oh, hello Professor Parsons."

Rick's attention was still on the police cruiser in the background, and the girl swiveled her head in the direction he gazed. "What's with the police?" she said, turning her eyes once more to Peg.

"The police," Peg replied innocently. "You mean that patrol car?" She shrugged slightly. "Professor Parsons here and I were just wondering the same thing. Right Professor Parsons?"

Rick suddenly realized he was being addressed. "What's that, Peg? Sorry about that. Hey there Julia, how are you doing?"

"I was just about to tell Julia here that the police sometimes send an official over when we're doing equipment certs." She saw the blank look on Rick's face and gave him a subtle glance. "Isn't that what we both thought?"

"Certification?" said Rick, finally understanding her meaning. "Yes, that's it. Certification." He turned to face the student, his expression becoming more relaxed. "A couple times during the summer we have to have the State do a standards certification on some of the more advanced lab equipment, and they usually send someone from Cheboygan to assist with the evaluation."

Julia nodded as if the explanation made perfect sense, and Rick felt slightly guilty at the deception. "Whatever you say," she replied.

"Are you working in the upper woods this afternoon?" said Peg, wanting to direct the subject away from the nearby cruiser.

She shook her head and reached over her shoulder to tap the backpack. "Not today. I just bought two field books, though. Professor Evans said we'd need one for tomorrow, since we'll be on the ridge east of Pine Point."

"Ah, that's right," said Peg, her eyes narrowing slightly as an idea occurred to her. "Tanner switched his lecture sessions with your group so you'd have consecutive field days. Did your class meet in the upper lab this morning?"

The girl nodded. "We did. In fact, we just let out before I came here to get the supplies." She smiled and glanced shyly in the narrow space between where Peg and Rick stood. "Do you mind if I pass through you? I'm on my way back up the hill to the can."

Rick couldn't help but chuckle at her phrasing. An outsider would think she somewhat crudely referred to the bathroom, however he knew she meant what the upper row students lovingly called their tin-sided small dorms. The "cans" were a line of two-person shacks on the hill above the lakeside lab, notoriously hot in the summer and promising nothing more than rustic accommodations. Students did their best to personalize their own can, often decorating the front doors with various styles of hippie art, and hanging hammocks outside between the nearby trees. They reminded Rick of the living quarters in the episodes of the television series M.A.S.H.

The pair stepped aside as Julia started between them along the sidewalk. "I actually need to contact Professor Evans, Julia," Peg said. "Did he happen to mention to your class whether or not he had plans for the rest of the day?"

The girl shrugged. "We just let out twenty minutes ago. He's probably still up there if you want to catch him." With that, she turned and began walking to the far side.

"That explains it," said Peg to Rick after the girl vanished around the corner and ascended the small trail into the trees. "The cell coverage stinks in the lab –"

"If Tanner even has his cell," he added.

"Well, apart from Prima Donna," she continued and then amended in light of the circumstance. "I mean, aside from Peter and Tanner, I've been able to get in touch with everybody else."

"And Sondra?" said Rick, wondering if she

qualified as official station faculty or staff.

As if Peg read his thoughts, she replied, "I wasn't sure whether or not to contact her. Charles didn't specify, so I gave it my best shot, and no, I couldn't reach her either." She glanced at her watch and then looked up to find Rick gesturing across the volleyball court toward Heather, who approached the administration building from the direction of the shore road. "Tell you what. We're supposed to meet in fifteen minutes. Would you mind going to the upper lab to see if Tanner is there and tell him about the meeting? I'll intercept Heather and escort her to the main room."

Rick watched for a moment longer then nodded. "I'll go see if I can find him."

Chapter 10

The group waited uneasily as Charles finished speaking privately with a woman seated next to him. Heather recognized her as one of the Alliance administrators who had attended Sondra's project update over a week ago, and unlike the confident persona she displayed then, her face now bore an expression of deep concern. Even Charles, who most regarded affectionately as a laid back leftover hippie, looked uncharacteristically distraught. Strands of silver hair had escaped his ponytail and hung in disorderly strands across his neck. He nodded gravely and then motioned to the back of the room, where Officer Bennett waited impassively near the main entry door.

The assembly watched stoically as Officer Bennett pushed the door slowly shut, turned and then walked up the side aisle to the front table.

"Right then," said Charles, which several in the audience would otherwise have found amusing under different circumstances, as he was well known to begin his lectures and meetings with this simple greeting. "Look, I know calling a sudden meeting like this is most unusual, and I apologize for it." He paused and slowly scanned his colleagues' faces, before turning his eyes to the entry door. As he did so, Heather took a quick inventory of those seated in the room, and her eyes found Rick's face staring back at her from across the row. She mouthed silently,

"Where's Peter?" receiving nothing more than a returned shrug.

Charles' delay was interrupted as Abigail stopped beside him, clearly implying that he was to relinquish control.

"The thing is," he continued, "we have a situation here which requires Officer Bennett's presence, and I think it's best now for me to turn things over to her so she can give you an update on how the County wishes to proceed."

Again, Heather glanced at Rick and saw the same confusion as her own mirrored on his face.

"Thank you, Dr. Henderson," Abigail began, nodding to him in a way that suggested he take a seat next to Caroline Cox. She then looked directly at Peg, who sat off to the side. "Were you able to contact everyone?"

If Peg was intimidated by the official circumstances, it didn't show. She did a quick scan about the room to make sure someone hadn't slipped in unnoticed, pausing as she spied Peter's graduate student near the back. "Wasn't able to locate Professor Cummings, but I suspect he may be out on the branch. Is that right, Elise?"

The young woman twitched as though she'd been given an electric jolt. "Um, yes. I think Peter ... I mean Professor Cummings was going to be out on the river for the better part of the afternoon."

Peg's eyes narrowed slightly as if she was weighing the response, then she turned to face Abigail. "There's almost zero cell reception south of Robinson Road, where Professor Cummings' main site is located by the river. If he's there, and I bet he is, it's a dead zone."

Rick saw Charles noticeably wince at her choice of words.

"Ok," Abigail continued. "Anyone else?"

"Couple of doc assistants and our maintenance

staff."

"And Sondra," blurted Monica, seated beside Heather.

With that, Charles again paled visibly.

Abigail nodded curtly to Peg and readdressed the group. "I've been called in to investigate what may be a missing person's case." She paused to carefully gauge the various reactions. "Has anyone here had any contact with Dr. Parker within the past two days?"

Heads turned to one another, and no one spoke for several seconds. Rick's mind recalled the image of the white station truck speeding out of the Grapevine Point Woods, and he turned around in his seat to face Monica, his expression enough that she uneasily broke the silence.

"Shall I tell them –" she insisted quickly, before Abigail cut her off by silencing her with a raised palm.

"Thank you, Monica. Give me a moment to ask a few preliminary questions before I invite you to describe your experience from today. Is that clear?"

Monica merely nodded.

"I'll assume for now that none of you have seen or heard from Dr. Parker in the past two days. I'm to understand that Dr. Parker received some equipment from you a couple days ago and that she intended to do some research related to the Alliance project?"

Again Monica nodded, clearly confused whether she was to elaborate or not. Rick, who was still turned slightly in his seat, found her reticence amusing. He'd never known Monica not to speak her mind.

Abigail recognized the woman's dilemma. "Was there anything you'd like to add about that exchange?"

Monica suddenly remembered herself, raising her voice slightly. "Sondra needed the temperature probes for her work on the East Branch, so I assisted her in checking them out."

"And this was how long ago?"

"In the morning. Two days ago."

All heads turned to Tanner, who raised his hand slightly and said in a calm voice. "Excuse me, Officer Bennett. It seems none of us here have seen Sondra in the past couple days. Forgive me for being rude, but would you mind telling us why you think she is officially missing?"

If his directness bothered her, Abigail's face showed no change in composure. "And you are?"

"Tanner Evans. I'm one of the faculty here."

Abigail turned to Caroline Cox and nodded.

Caroline took a deep breath and stared fixedly at her hands placed before her on the table. "Sondra and I were supposed to meet yesterday evening at dinner to discuss her ongoing work with the project. Our group operates out of Gaylord, and I have been in almost daily contact with Sondra via email or text messages. I last spoke with her two days ago, when we confirmed our dinner plans." She looked up from the table. "That was the last communication I had with her. No phone, email, text. Nothing since."

"I assume someone has already checked her cabin here?" inquired Rick.

Charles lifted his hand from the table as if to signal permission to speak. "When Caroline contacted me this morning and told me of her concerns, I personally went down to Dr. Parker's residence to look around. Nothing appeared out of the ordinary, though admittedly I don't know Sondra all that well." He frowned slightly, realizing the awkwardness of his statement. "I should say, her place was tidy, and there was no sign of her or anything to suggest that she was somewhere close by, like a cell phone or keys on the table. That sort of thing."

"What about her car?" said Heather. Though the

faculty cabins were situated along the shoreline and fronted by a narrow dirt road, there was a separate parking area on a parallel road roughly a hundred feet set back into the woods.

"It was sitting there next to everyone else's." replied Charles. He used a free hand to push the errant strands of hair back over his ear and tucked them within the elastic band holding his ponytail. "I went to find Peg at the Admin Building to see if she knew anything about Sondra's whereabouts."

Peg leaned back in her chair and folded her arms across her chest. "All I knew was that Sondra was planning to do readings out on the branch this week, starting near the lake and working upstream."

Abigail turned to face Elise. "You work with Dr. Cummings?"

"Yes."

"And his site is also on the East Branch?"

"Yes."

Rick noticed a slight change in expression on Abigail's face, registering the barest hint of frustration with Elise's less than forthcoming responses.

"And when is the last time you spoke with him?"

Elise leaned forward suddenly, her voice an octave higher. "Why all the questions about Dr. Cummings and me! Yes, he works on the East Branch! No, I do not work at that particular site! He has me doing species identifications along the West Branch, which is several miles away."

Abigail's face still showed little emotion. "Ms.?"

Elise suddenly became aware the room had gone quiet and that she was the sole focus of everyone's attention. She composed herself and spoke softly as before. "Sheppard. Elise Sheppard."

"Fine. Ms. Sheppard. Let me stress at this point, I

am simply trying to get a general account of everyone's whereabouts. Since you work with Dr. Cummings, in the likelihood that he had made contact with Dr. Parker in the past two days, perhaps he may have shared something with you?"

Elise shook her head slowly. "I haven't even seen him myself for a while."

"And a while is how long exactly?"

The young woman lowered her voice uncertainly. "The day before last. Like I said, I've been working alone along the upper reaches of the west branch."

Satisfied with this response, Abigail gave her a cursory nod before turning once again to Monica.

"Why don't you describe for the group what happened this morning."

Monica hesitated, taking her eyes from Officer Bennett and glancing quickly to Charles, who smiled slightly and tilted his head as if to offer both his blessing and encouragement. Then, to his surprise, she fixed her gaze on Rick and began to speak.

"Charles contacted me earlier this morning to ask if I'd seen Sondra ... er ... Dr. Parker recently. I was down in the main lab doing prep work for one of Rick's classes when he rang my cell."

Rick cast a quick glance at Abigail and found her regarding him appraisingly, much in the same way she did over a week ago in this same place.

"I told Charles I hadn't seen Dr. Parker for a day or so, that she was using some of the old temp probes out on the East to do her gradient analysis. He then told me someone was having difficulty getting in touch with Dr. Parker and that nobody seemed to know exactly where she was. He asked if I'd be willing to take one of the station trucks out to the access road off Robinson and see if I could find her."

"Go on," said Abigail, who found it curious how Monica's attention was still fixed on Rick in the seat in front of her.

"I took the truck by the lab and went down Riggsville toward Pellston. Plains Road intersects near the bottom of the hill where Riggsville turns into Robinson, and one of the access tracks to the river is about a quarter mile down Plains."

"That's where Peter goes in." offered Peg.

"I actually passed his truck on my way in," replied Monica. "The two track is pretty wide where it first goes into the woods, and there's a pull out spot off the side maybe a couple hundred yards in where it gets a little sandy. I knew that was Peter's truck, so I passed by and continued on."

"It gets rough after that," said Rick, picturing the point after the pull out where the two track narrows as it enters into more dense woods.

"Yeah, tell me about it. Grass in the berm between the tracks was high and kept smacking the bottom of the truck after that point." Monica paused and winced slightly, looking to Charles. "I probably scratched the hell out of the truck from the branches."

Charles simply waved his hand dismissively.

"How far?" said Abigail.

"Maybe a quarter mile on," said Monica. "The two track follows the Maple's flow, though you'd never know it. The understory's so thick you don't see the river. I seriously doubt that stretch gets much use. Anyway, I came to the second pull out, and there was another white station truck parked right there off the side. The road dead ends after that a while further, so I pulled past the truck to a spot where I could do a three point between two trees, and I shut it off."

"Was it Sondra's?" said Heather unexpectedly,

causing everyone to turn in her direction. "Sorry to interrupt. You were saying?"

"The driver's door was unlocked. There was an Alliance folder on the passenger seat with a bunch of paperwork." Monica met Heather's eyes. "It was her truck."

"I'm sorry," Rick interjected. "There has to be something more than this. So, you came across the station truck she used. There's a gap here between finding the truck and a missing person."

"It was the smell," Monica blurted, which for a fraction of a second made Rick think of a dead body, and he almost said so, until he thankfully remembered the part about the missing person. "There was a small lunch cooler on the passenger floor. You know, one of those Igloo things. My God, the smell was pretty rancid." Her face scrunched as she recalled the odor. "I opened it, and inside floating in a pool of water was what looked like a tuna sandwich gone bad in a Ziploc bag."

Rick glanced to Abigail. "How long would it take?"

She gave him the barest hint of a smile. "Do you mean for it to go bad?"

Rick nodded.

"A day. Maybe less. It would have taken several hours for the ice to melt completely. After that, in a hot car, perhaps twelve hours." Abigail regarded Monica again. "And the trail?"

"There's a small single track that runs from the pull out through the woods to the river. I closed the truck – " she paused and looked at her, "I didn't lock it. Was that ok?"

"It's fine," said Abigail.

"So I closed the door and started up the trail. The ferns were pretty thick along the way, and I could tell someone had been through there recently from the broken ones here and there. Plus, there were strands of spider webs between the trees, which kept hitting my face as I walked. So, assuming Sondra had gone to the river that way, it must have been a while since she passed through."

Rick admired her little bit of deduction, thinking himself of the times he'd hiked through the Grapevine Point trails in the morning and knew someone had gone before him from the absence of spider web strands.

"The path goes for a hundred yards or so until it comes to the Maple. There's a place on the bank where sand has collected near the trail end. The river's a little wider there, maybe thirty feet across, and I could see places in the sandy bottom where someone had entered from the trail and walked upstream a ways." When she finished speaking, Monica compressed her lips in a thin line and shook her head in bewilderment.

"And how far up river is it to Peter's site?" asked Heather. The implication wasn't lost on several in the group, and Rick noticed David wince slightly.

"It can't be that far," replied Monica. "I'm not really all that sure. The river curves around and gets narrow as it goes – "

"It's not far," interrupted Elise. She gave Heather a withering look. "But what's the point with your question?"

Heather raised her hands submissively. "Nothing. Just trying to get a sense of things. I'm not trying to suggest –"

"Do you know that stretch between the trail and Dr. Cumming's site?" Abigail asked Elise.

Elise regarded her coolly before responding. "I've walked the river from his site almost all the way to Lake Kathleen. It's maybe a tenth a mile between where Sondra would have entered and Peter's, though like she said the river gets narrow and winds around. There are spots that are almost impossible to walk through, with deep holes and deadfalls."

Abigail addressed Monica again. "I assume you tried shouting her name."

Monica nodded. "I yelled as loud as I could. There was no response."

"And then you drove back here?"

Again she nodded.

"What about Peter's truck?" said Rick. "You said you saw his truck on the way in, right? You didn't stop to try to find Peter? Maybe he'd seen her."

Monica let her words come quickly, clearly uncomfortable with the question. "I know! I can't explain it. I should have stopped." She looked from Rick to the others and settled on Abigail. "I guess I just panicked a little, from what I saw in her truck and not finding her at the river. I ... I just came back here and found Peg and Charles, and well, now you know the rest."

"Which is why I've asked Monica to take me to the site once we've finished here," said Abigail. "She and I will go see if we can locate Dr. Cummings and find out if he knows anything. If that's the case, of course we hope for a reasonable explanation for her whereabouts. Otherwise, I'm going to have to plan for a formal search, and I will likely need your assistance, especially those of you familiar with the local terrain." With that, she turned to Charles. "In the mean time, there's not much you all can do, though I expect you to treat this situation confidentially until we know more."

"I think we should inform the students," he said.

Abigail shook her head. "Not at this stage." She then regarded the assembly once again. "I know you have a rather close knit community, and I suspect there is already talk about our unscheduled emergency meeting. I suggest you simply tell curious students that the station has been contacted for an unscheduled inspection of the facilities –

something that required an immediate action from all staff. I'd leave it at that for the time being." She then used her hand to beckon Monica. "Why don't you show me the river access site, and we'll see if we can find Dr. Cummings."

Chapter 11

"Hey! Hold up, will you?"

Rick turned to find Heather walking quickly toward him on the road. Her shoes scuffled in the dry gravel, creating small clouds of dust that drifted away in the breeze from off the lake.

"I didn't know you were going this way," he said.

"I don't have anything until later this afternoon, when I'm supposed to meet with two students back in the library." She gestured ahead to their cabins. "You going home?"

"I guess so," Rick replied absently. "I wasn't sure what else to do after that meeting."

Heather fell into step beside him and glanced at her watch as they approached the row of faculty housing. "You want to talk about it? I can make us both a sandwich, and we could sit on the back porch, if you like."

Rick didn't respond initially, and as they passed Peter's cabin he looked outward toward the water, distracted as a Kingfisher swooped along the shore from the boughs of one overhanging pine to the next. His eyes met hers then, and he nodded meaningfully toward the end of the shore road past the last cottage. "Do you mind if we go for a walk first?" He laughed softly, seeing a look of hesitation on her face. "Sorry. I'm not trying to avoid lunch with you. A sandwich sounds great. I just feel like being in the woods for awhile after all that."

The road came to an end at the forest edge, where a small driveway angled left toward the shore and emptied at the front of a large a-frame house. A small wooden placard near the entry door read "Director's Residence."

"Charles looked pretty shaken, don't you think?" Rick said as they took a connecting path to the trail.

"I guess."

"You guess?"

Heather fell in behind him as they approached the entrance to the single track, leading north into the woods between the fishtail bays. "Yeah, I guess. I mean, of course he's upset with the possibility of Sondra missing and all. And you know he doesn't like formal meetings, especially something of an emergency."

The trail opened before them in a straight line through the thick woods, and Rick slowed slightly to allow Heather a chance to catch up. The bright sunshine from the dusty road was replaced by softer hues of filtered greens from the foliage above, where a mixture of hardwoods and conifers towered overhead in a cathedral of northern woods. Their footfalls went softly on the carpet of brown pine needles as they walked slowly ahead.

"I still don't understand your 'I guess' part."

"Well, I bet Charles is a little relieved to turn things over to the police. What's her name again?"

"Bennett," Rick said. "I met her briefly that night of the Alliance presentation."

"I remember seeing her there. She stood over near the side of the lecture hall the whole time."

Rick nodded. "Until there was a little altercation at the end, and that's when she came over to where I was seated."

Heather recalled him telling her about this after it happened. "Didn't you say she was called in to attend that meeting, because there was the potential for trouble?"

The path angled slightly to the left and rose several feet up a small crest, where the canopy thinned briefly to allow shafts of direct sunlight to penetrate the forest floor. Rick pointed to the base of a nearby white cedar, where the speckled red cap of a mushroom poked upward from among the carpet of needles.

"Fly agaric?" he said, looking to her for confirmation.

"Beats me," she replied. "I'm the pollen scientist, remember?"

He chuckled softly, distracted momentarily from their discussion. "I think it is Amanita something or other. Remind me to ask Tanner next time we see him."

For a moment, she thought about pressing him on his use of the word 'we' but decided instead to enjoy her own interpretation.

"You remember that guy in the audience who was a little antagonistic about the project?"

"That's right. You were telling me about this the other night with Peter."

"Yeah. Though I'd kind of brushed it off then, apart from getting a little kick out of seeing Peter becoming worked up in the lab."

Heather stepped over a downed white birch that had fallen across the path. She pulled a large branch to the side to clear the way for him to follow.

"Thanks," he said as he passed through and waited until she cautiously released the limb to rejoin him.

"Well, it looks like trouble has come after all, unless this morning's been just a big misunderstanding."

They continued on silently for several minutes, each privately working through the sequence of events from the past several days. Ahead, the trail approached a small gate, where beyond a two-track cut across the way. To the left, it descended gradually for a hundred feet before petering out in a grassy opening near a break in the forest on the eastern shore. To the right, it climbed sharply uphill and curved out of sight into the deep woods.

The pair skirted a narrow gap between one of the gateposts and the trunk of a nearby white pine then turned left to follow the track to the lake's edge. In the small clearing were the remains of charred logs, set within a crude circle of stones among the sandy soil. Rick gestured to two large trees on the periphery a dozen feet away, where several faded straps of webbing encircled loosely around the trunks.

"Those have been there since I can remember."

Heather walked over and grabbed one of the worn pieces in her hand, smiling suddenly as she turned to him. "Straps for hammocks?"

"That's it." He motioned around the clearing with an outstretched hand. "When I was growing up here in the summer we used to come down to this very spot to party. We'd build a fire and drink beer and hang around in hammocks."

"Surely not between these trees," she teased, holding the webbing up for him to see. "These would have been just saplings if they were even around at all."

He smiled at her as he used his foot to poke at several of the charred logs. "Be nice, will you. Looks like someone's been carrying on that tradition recently."

Heather released the straps and walked slowly across the clearing to a spot where the berm spilled gently onto a narrow strip of sandy beach. The expanse of water lay before her, glistening from the sun's reflection upon countless breaking waves that traveled down the length until they emptied softly on the shoals that formed the eastern shore. She motioned for him to join her, and together they sat amid the puzzle grass and wild mint and warm sand. Overhead several terns glided lazily across the shoal, hunting for perch and occasionally diving suddenly into the clear water. Rick let his eyes scan the distant shorelines, lost in the unspoiled beauty of the deep greens of the forest against the cerulean sky above and the shifting hues of the warm water. As he turned his head toward the near shore, he found her pulling absently at a piece of grass, strands of blonde hair waving disobediently across her face from the breeze.

"Are you still here?"

She blinked and shifted her gaze to his face, taking a deep breath of the northern air. "It smells a little like back home."

"As in England home?" he asked uncertainly.

"No," she laughed softly. "Maine. Well, I guess that's only my academic home, but still, in many ways this place reminds me of back there." She took another deep breath and exhaled slowly as she grasped a handful of soft sand a let it spill gently from her fingers. "Except the water smells different."

"Not exactly the ocean smell?"

She took another handful of sand, this one containing a tiny cylindrical shaped white shell. She used fingers of her other hand to grasp it and reached over toward him holding it forth. "What's this called again?"

He took it in his palm and studied it absently in the direct sunlight. "Elimia livescens. It's basically a freshwater snail." He handed it gently back to her. "My poor students get to know these things pretty exhaustively during the term."

"I know," she demurred sheepishly.

Rick arched an eyebrow.

"The students call you the algae snail guy," she added, placing her hand over her mouth to stifle a laugh.

"Well, I guess there could be worse things than algae guy or Professor pond scum."

Heather coughed as she tried to contain a muffled laugh, then she noticed his suggestive expression. "Wait," she said suddenly. "When you say it could be worse, do you mean something about me?"

Now it was his turn to laugh. "They promised me not to say anything, Heather." He laughed again when he saw her eyes widen. "I'm only kidding. Actually, the general gossip about you is pretty positive. Makes me envious."

A whining noise out on the water caught their attention, and they both turned to watch as a speedboat full of teenagers cut a wide arc from the direction of north fishtail toward the shallow water of the big shoal. Behind in its wake was a young girl holding on to the sides of a large inner tube, being whiplashed in tow across the waves. The boat turned sharply, sending the tube flying in the opposite direction, all the while the passengers yelled happily. The pair followed it as it sped across the drop off and veered toward the distant point where the Grapevine Point woods lay beyond the shore. Rick raised his finger and pointed just to the left, drawing her attention to a slow-moving pontoon that cut lazily through the water on its return to the station.

"Was that you years ago?" Heather asked softly, watching his gaze shift back and forth between the two boats.

"Yeah. I guess it was. I told you we were a bunch of yahoos." He then nodded to the retreating pontoon. "I wonder if those kids on the speedboat make fun of the Bug Campers like we used to do?"

"You said before not much has changed."

He turned to face her then, aware that he had forgotten the troubling events from earlier and grateful she was here with him to share this place. "Look, Heather, I um –"

She sensed where this was headed and knew under the circumstances the timing wasn't right, even though she shared his feelings. "I suppose we ought to talk more about what happened before," she interrupted, watching as he reacted uncertainly. "Rick, don't misunderstand. This is lovely here, and I'm glad we came. This certainly beats lunch on the porch. I hope you and I can come back here again soon, just the two of us, ok?"

He nodded slightly and then changed the subject back to more neutral ground. "Have you ever been to that part of the Maple?"

Heather blinked several times, trying to refocus on the meeting. "No, and actually, I've never been on any part of the Maple."

"At all?" Rick blurted disbelievingly then softened as it occurred to him she likely had no good reason for going there. "Someday I'll have to take you to one of the wider stretches, below the dam. You can put a kayak in and go for quite a ways. It's just beautiful."

"What about on the branch?"

"You've seen Lake Kathleen, right?"

"Only when I've eaten at the Lake Site." Another thought occurred to her. "Hold it. Once I took the back road home from the restaurant. The one that cuts along the lake beneath the dam."

"Woodland Road," he offered.

"I guess so." She used her hands to gesture as if giving directions along a curving road. "It bends around after the dam and heads east, I think. Goes for a while and comes to an intersection. I went left there and drove a couple miles until I hit Robinson Road."

"That's it," Rick said encouragingly.

"What's it?"

"That road. The one from the intersection. Right before you came to Robinson, there would have been a couple sandy two tracks that cut west into the woods. You probably didn't even see them when you were driving, unless you were trying to find them."

The realization came to her, and Heather's voice raised slightly. "That's where Sondra went into the river."

"And Peter."

"Even along the road, I remember it being pretty remote there."

Rick nodded. "It's worse when you go into the woods. It's not exactly a maintained stretch of road. More like an old forest trail."

"But didn't Monica say it was fairly open for the first part?"

"It is," Rick said, "only because Peter's been using it pretty frequently for a couple years to access his site up stream."

Heather's brow wrinkled slightly. "Then why does the road even continue on?"

"Probably for DNR access, but I suspect it's hardly ever used by them. Plus, there are sport fishermen who sometimes take the road to get to the upper stretches."

"Like the guy from the other night."

Rick recalled the threatening image of Mike Pritchard standing over him in the lecture hall. "Yeah, like him."

"But didn't you say the river's fairly closed in on the upper part? How could anyone do any fishing there? In fact, why would anyone want to?"

"Probably for the same sort of reasons why anyone would want to study endangered plants, or diatom distributions, or pollen assemblages. Need I say more."

She arched an eyebrow. "Meaning?"

He reached for a small pebble on the sand and tossed it gently into the water near the shore, startling a school of small minnows that was feeding in the shallows of the sunlit sandy bottom. They darted away quickly and circled back lazily to the same place. "Meaning that a passion is a passion, I guess. Yes, it gets pretty congested in there, but I doubt it matters all that much if it's simply a part of what you enjoy doing." He took another pebble and tossed it absently. "I once tried walking a stretch of the Maple."

She looked at him questioningly.

"A little further up. You know that spot on Douglas Lake Road where the Maple goes underneath through a culvert?"

"There's a little pull out next to the road for parking."

"That's it. Peter sometimes takes his Limnology Class there for river fieldwork. They pile into one of the vans and spend a few hours in that spot doing measurements."

"And you went from there?"

"Started there and went downstream. It looked open from the road. The land is gentle and the river is fairly wide there, but let me tell you it gets choked a hundred feet into the woods. It curves this way and that, sometimes opening up in a shallow pool maybe twenty feet across and a foot deep. Mostly it's closed in. There are deadfalls across nearly ever fifty feet, and the trees arc overhead. It gets deep in spots too. I'd come to a place where the river eddied around a bend, and it would all of a sudden get four feet deep."

She tried to imagine what it was like wading through the narrow stretches, stooping beneath branches and stepping over fallen debris. "Well, at least you had it to yourself," she said drily.

"Except for the mosquitoes and deer flies."

"And now you've given me a new respect for Peter's research site."

Rick nodded. "He's in a spot that's a little more open, but not much. There's a small access trail along the river, which is more like a deer trail, that runs from where he parks up to the bank and past his site."

Heather turned to him. "Deer trail or fisherman trail?"

"Both I guess, plus researcher trail. It's one and the same in that remote spot." He smiled ruefully. "I didn't get very far. I got out of the river and bushwhacked east. There's a good two track that runs north/south alongside, and I popped out onto it and walked back to where I had parked my car."

"And this is the same Maple River you think I should experience."

"I don't mean there! That is, unless you want to go see for yourself. Like I said before, below the dam, the river really opens up. Both branches empty into Lake Kathleen, and the flow over the spillway is enough to keep the volume high in the lower stretches as it gets toward Burt Lake."

"And people fish the lower part?"

"Most of the fly fishing takes place below the dam. It's more open and better stocked. There are some lake fish that migrate in. Hidden River operates not too far downstream."

"Hidden River, the golf course?"

"And fly fishing outfitter. They kind of have a monopoly in the lower section, which is why guys like Mike Pritchard tend to pick and choose in the less accessible places upstream."

Heather nodded absently, her mind working through a tenuous thread of possibilities. "What about the lake?"

Rick's face registered confusion. "What about it?"

"That's right, I've seen them there before."

"You've lost me."

"The boats. On Lake Kathleen. I've seen plenty of small fishing boats on the lake when I've eaten at the Lake Site."

Rick gave her a pleading look. "I'm still not following you –"

"Just thinking through Sondra's presentation the other night. You just mentioned Mike Pritchard, and that made me recall seeing the owner of the Lake Site in the audience too. What's his name again?"

"Miles. Miles Kirnan. Why?"

"So, it's no wonder there was concern about the meeting getting confrontational." Heather's eyes narrowed as she tried to reimagine the view from her table at the Lake Site. "That's public access."

"You mean Lake Kathleen?"

Heather nodded.

"I don't think so. In fact, I'm pretty sure it's not. The Kirnans used to own most of the acreage down the hill from the restaurant, including the lake, however they sold most of land several years ago. There's a couple cabins tucked back on the eastern side, accessible off Woodland Road. I remember Miles telling me a few years ago the new owners rent them out during the summer. My guess is the boats you've seen are from renters."

Heather inhaled softly and tilted her head meaningfully. "Huh. I suspect he's not exactly a fan of the project going forward. Will the lake be completely drained?"

"Most likely. The river will return to its natural course through the basin, with the west and east branches coming together and flowing down to the lower course. Once the lake's gone, it's going to look scoured for a while, maybe a year or two, but it won't take long for succession to establish things fairly quickly."

"I don't think that will be much comfort to the Kirnans."

Rick shrugged his shoulders. "I imagine Miles was hoping for better news the other night."

"Or maybe someone to come to his defense?"

"Like I said that night, I'm staying neutral on the whole thing."

Heather kept silent for several seconds, weighing her own feelings about the project. Her thoughts then turned to the meeting an hour ago. "What do you think about Monica's discovery?"

"It doesn't look good," he replied evenly. "Hopefully it's a big misunderstanding as you put it before, but from the little I know of working with Sondra, she didn't exactly strike me as someone who would go off line without a reason."

"What about how Elise acted?"

"What do you mean?"

"I just thought she seemed a bit defensive."

"Maybe," Rick said. "I guess it's a little strange how Peter seemed to banish her –"

"Coincidentally. And during the time when Sondra goes missing," Heather interrupted softly, almost tentatively.

Rick's eyes jerked toward hers and held them. "Don't you think that's a stretch?"

Heather didn't look away. "Don't tell me it didn't cross your mind."

His face softened as he exhaled through pursed lips. "Ok. I admit I did think the timing was a bit odd." He mouth then formed a slight smile as another thought occurred.

"What?" Heather demanded, surprised at his subtle change.

"It's not nice," he replied, trying to stifle a small laugh.

"What?" she said again, her voice raising slightly.

"Just that, you'd think anybody, particularly a graduate student, would be happy to be separated from Peter for more than twenty four hours."

Heather smiled knowingly and was about to reply, when they both heard voices approaching from the connecting trail. A pair of students, a boy and girl, descended from the grassy berm and onto the connecting beach, hand in hand. The boy gave a sharp cry of surprise as he nearly stumbled into Rick.

"Oh my God! I'm so sorry." He sheepishly released the girl's hand and glanced furtively back and forth between Heather and Rick. "We didn't think anyone would be out here."

Rick brushed the sand off his legs as he stood then reached over to take Heather's hand to help her up. The young girl's face blushed with recognition, and she gave a tentative wave as a greeting. "Hey Professor Wilkins."

Heather smiled kindly, and still holding onto Rick's hand, she led him past the newcomers and toward the berm. "It's all yours, Stacey," she said. "This is a perfect spot for some peace and quiet." She then gave the girl a meaningful look, adding "and privacy."

Words tumbled out of the girl's mouth. "I'm so sorry Professor! We didn't think anyone would be way out here."

Heather laughed softly. "We were just leaving anyway." She glanced to the boy, who charmingly seemed embarrassed at having their privacy disturbed. "Tell you what," she said to the pair, her expression a little mischievous. "We won't tell, if you don't, ok?"

The girl simply nodded, and Heather led Rick up the path into the eastern woods. She fell beside him on the path, still holding his hand. "Out with the old, and in with the new?"

He chuckled softly, enjoying the feel of her warm hand in his. "Not so old," he replied as they walked southward back toward the camp.

Chapter 12

Jan eyed the group of teenagers as they entered the door and shuffled over to an empty table in the corner. She gave Rick a knowing smile and downed the remaining few sips of coffee, saying discreetly to him as she jerked her head in their direction, "There's us, twenty some years ago."

He glanced over and watched as the three boys and two girls chatted loudly, their conversation peppered with a southern dialect he couldn't quite place. "I think I've seen them here before, right?"

Jan struggled to lift her plump frame and quickly smoothed the front of her apron. "Yeah. Those kids are regulars from out Douglas way." She followed his gaze and listened as one of the boys challenged another to eating the full stack of blueberry pancakes. "They come in at least twice a week."

Rick raised his eyebrows in a way that suggested empathy, and she chuckled softly.

"No, they're good kids, mostly. Kinda like we used to be ... mostly." She pulled an order pad from a front pocket and started over toward the table. "Be back shortly, and you can fill me in on the news." Rick watched her for a few moments as she deftly greeted the bunch and joked with them as they ordered far more food than they could possibly eat.

"You can get your own refill Erasmus," she called

to him, gesturing with a free hand toward the pots near the open kitchen. Hearing his name elicited a few snickers from the teens, and Rick simply ignored them as he stood and walked over to the waiting pot, his eyes catching a glimpse of a discarded stack of Mike Pritchard's advertisements in a pile on a nearby shelf. He grabbed one and turned it over in his hand, recognizing it as the same flier displayed on the table over a week ago.

Jan passed him on the way to the kitchen and noticed the curious expression on his face as he held it up for her to see. "Oh, I'll tell you about that in a moment after I post this order." She rolled her eyes. "I'll be damned if they eat everything."

Rick put the advertisement back, filled his cup and returned to the table, grateful the Deli was relatively empty at this time of day, apart from the teens who continued to talk over one another in a noisy fashion. It didn't seem that long ago, he thought to himself, when he ran around with a similar group, enjoying carefree adventures only the lake and the long days of summer could provide. He smiled then, and took a long sip of coffee as he watched as one of the boys secretly tear a sugar packet and dump the contents into the younger of the two girl's glass of orange juice.

Jan rejoined him and pulled a seat toward the table, saying to what appeared to be the oldest nearby, "Your order should be ready in about ten minutes or so. Let me know if you need anything in the meantime." Then she deposited herself abruptly in the chair and regarded Rick with an inquisitive face. "Any word on her whereabouts?"

Charles had made it clear two days ago the staff was to keep the upmost confidentiality about Sondra's disappearance and the ongoing search conducted by the Cheboygan Police. Had it been anyone else inquiring,

Rick's face would have registered surprise. With Jan, however, he knew well enough she had connections about local happenings. "Should've figured you already knew," he said drily. "I'm surprised they haven't enlisted you to spearhead the search in some way, given how you know nearly everyone in Emmet County."

"And Cheboygan," she beamed. Jan glanced upward to one of several topographic maps that adorned the paneled wall, her eyes fixing on an image of the inland lakes waterway depicting several river basins with the Maple River watershed. "How many days?" she said simply.

"Three."

She exhaled slowly and regarded him once again. "No leads at all?"

"I might as well ask you the same thing. I suspect you've been talking to Peg, but I won't incriminate either of you by pressing it, so don't even bother to react."

Jan huffed a little. "It doesn't look good, that's for sure. I assume the Prima Donna came back into the fold."

"Yes. He returned to the station that evening of the day Officer Bennett made the announcement, and as far as I know he's stayed fairly close to the camp since."

"And what's the deal with that graduate student who works with him?"

Rick eyed her again appraisingly. "I really ought to say 'no comment'."

"Try to remember it's me, Erasmus."

"So why don't you tell me what I already know?" he teased.

"Maybe something fishy there," she said.

His eyes focused on the far wall behind her, where several large trout were displayed among various sizes of antique fishing lures and tackle. "What do you mean by fishy?"

"A romance."

His face twitched in surprise. "Hell no, Jan! With Peter?" His small outburst caught the attention of the teens, who had now turned silently toward him. "Sorry," Rick muttered to them as he lowered his voice. "From what I've heard, Peter treats her like a graduate slave more than anything. I suspect her own dissertation work dovetails with his research, so she has a vested interest in making sure nothing threatens Peter's site."

Jan tilted her head forward and looked up at him suggestively. "Which may or may not explain what I've been told about her defensiveness about him."

With that, Rick sat back in his chair and pulled his cup toward him to the edge of the table. "On that, I *do* have *no comment*." Once again his eyes drifted to the trophies on the far wall. "You were going to tell me something about Mike Pritchard?"

"He's had a bad accident."

"What do you mean?"

"Several days ago. His truck veered off the road coming back from Indian River. You know the four way at Vivio's Restaurant?"

Rick nodded, picturing the intersection where Route 68 headed west past the Cross In the Woods. "That cuts across toward Alanson?"

"Where it curves around Burt Lake, he evidently must have lost control and hit a tree on the side of the road."

"You're kidding me?" Rick whispered. "Is he going to be alright?"

Jan glanced over her shoulder toward the kitchen to see if the group's order was ready then turned back toward him. "He'll live, though he got a little banged up."

"How did you hear about it?"

She huffed softly. "From one of his clients. Guy from downstate came in here yesterday and saw the advertisements out on the table. I guess he'd hired Mike to take him fishing on the Maple, and he never showed. Evidently Mike called him from the hospital later that day to explain what had happened."

"Well he must not have been that badly injured if he was able to call," Rick replied.

"Evidently, he broke his collarbone when the truck's airbag deployed. And I guess he got several cuts on his face and took a good blow to the head. The truck was in bad shape from what I've heard."

"From the guy?"

A sly smile formed on her lips. "You know me better than that, Erasmus."

Rick's face showed a mixture of admiration and disapproval. "Your efficient network of Emmet County gossip."

She gave him a deep and throaty laugh. "Sort of. It's nothing too spicy. I know the owner of the shop where it's being worked on." Jan pointed to several of the empty tables. "Which is why I decided to remove the remaining fliers. Word has it Mike Pritchard will be off the river for a month or so."

"Well, I don't suppose you are too broken –" he started then paused as his cell phone gave a single chime. Rick reached into his pocket and glanced downward to check the screen. "Hmph," he muttered softly. "That's curious."

"What's the matter? Did you miss class or something, teach?" she teased gently.

"It's Heather." He glanced up, anticipating another goading comment. "This is odd."

Jan's face became more serious. "Trouble?"

"I'm not sure. The message just says "Emergency

meeting. Come back to the station ASAP."

"That can't be good."

"No. It doesn't look like it."

Jan nodded soberly. "Don't worry about settling up."

He held her eyes for a few moments and then stood quickly. "Thanks," he managed and added as he shifted toward the front door. "Talk soon, Jan."

"Good luck," she managed as she too stood and moved toward the kitchen.

#

Abigail Bennett stood in front of the assembled staff in the lecture hall. Rick glanced quickly around the room, experiencing a strange déjà vu moment, heightened by the curious fact that most everyone in attendance sat in nearly the same place as they did several days ago. That is, except for Charles, who occupied a chair in the front row next to one of the maintenance employees. Rick swiveled his head once again to the rear corner and found Peter and Elise next to one another.

"I believe we are all assembled," began Abigail.

"Except Tanner," piped in Peg, who then shriveled slightly when she saw the look of displeasure on Abigail's face at having been interrupted. "Sorry," she added softly.

"At eight o'clock this morning, a body was discovered in the south portion of Lake Kathleen by two fishermen. According to their statements, they were casting with weights, when one of their lures became entangled in something. When he pulled forcefully to extract the lure, it tore a piece of clothing, which remained embedded in the hook."

Rick glanced over at Heather, who regarded him with wide eyes and mouthed silently, "Oh my God."

"The water depth at that location was only twelve feet, and when the fishermen maneuvered their boat and peered downward, the angled sunlight was enough to reveal what appeared to be a human form resting on the bottom. The pair contacted the Emmet County Police Department, who were able to successfully retrieve the body. Having been appraised of the recent disappearance here at the Biological Station, Emmet County contacted my department in Cheboygan to assist with the identification and any possible investigation." Abigail paused and surveyed the room. "At this time, we have sufficient evidence to positively identify the remains as those of Dr. Sondra Parker."

Monica inhaled sharply, breaking the silence of the room. "Oh, how awful," she said softly.

"Also at this time, Emmet County has agreed to release jurisdiction of the remains to Cheboygan, and I will be leading the investigation. The body has been transferred to Cheboygan and is awaiting an autopsy." Abigail then glanced to Charles. "I've asked for the cooperation of the Director to allow my group full access to the facility and staff here in the upcoming days."

"That implies it wasn't exactly an accident!" blurted Peter, causing the assembly to turn toward him as one.

Abigail maintained her detached composure. "I ask you to refrain from speculation at this time, Dr. Cummings."

Being reprimanded in this way clearly upset Peter, compounded when he saw Monica regarding him furtively as she whispered something into Peg's ear.

"I'm not at liberty at this time to disclose anything beyond what I have already revealed. As the investigation unfolds, we will make any formal announcements as warranted. In the meantime, you are to do your best to conduct yourselves in a professional manner. You are, however, strictly forbidden to discuss this circumstance with anyone outside of this room. Furthermore, until such time as stated, you are to establish your whereabouts at all times with the Director, and you are to be in ready communication." As she finished speaking, her eyes rested plainly on Rick's face.

#

"I'd like a word with you, Dr. Parsons." The assembly had already begun to disperse, and as Rick started to follow Heather out the side door, he found Abigail standing beside him. Her pressed dark uniform with its shiny badge and other adornments stood notably in contrast to the others still filing out of the room. Rick stole a quick glance at her sidearm before finding her eyes. He sat back down and motioned for her to do the same in the chair beside him, grateful that she took the invitation instead of standing over him.

"Was that comment directed at me?" he said.

"Which comment?"

"About being in, how did you put it, ready communication."

Abigail frowned slightly, then allowed her face to relax. "No." She hesitated and surveyed the room to ensure they spoke privately. "Do you recall that I am an acquaintance of Jan Fowler?"

Realization dawned on him, and he eyed her cautiously. "You are concerned I may talk about this with Jan?"

"Worried isn't exactly the correct word, though I suppose that will do." Her eyes shifted to the exit door. "Give me a moment please." Before Rick had a chance to reply, she stood quickly and intercepted Charles as he was about to leave. The pair spoke softly for half a minute, and then she returned beside him once again. Apart from the two of them, the lecture hall had become empty.

"Look, Officer Bennett, let me make it clear that I will honor your request for confidentiality." His expression became slightly perturbed. "And frankly, I don't appreciate your implying otherwise."

"Relax, Professor," she replied. "It's not you I'm overly worried about. I've known Jan for a long time, and she has a way of ferreting information out of the most closemouthed and unsuspecting people."

"Then why are we sitting here?"

"Because I watched you closely the night of Dr. Parker's presentation. I saw how you handled yourself with impartiality and self control. Admittedly, out of curiosity I did some checking up on you with our mutual friend."

Rick's eyes widened slightly.

"It's nothing like that, I assure you," she added. "Call it professional curiosity. I'm taking a slight leap of faith now based on Jan's recommendation, and also from the fact that I've established with Charles your basic whereabouts the past several days."

"Look," he said again. "I'm really not following – "

"As things progress in the investigation, I may possibly need some inside assistance here within the camp."

"Me?" he said incredulously. "You are asking for *my* help?"

"I said possibly," she replied earnestly.

He remained silent for a moment, thinking over this unexpected request. "Her death was no accident."

Abigail regarded him critically. "No."

Rick exhaled slowly and used a free hand to rub his forehead. "Who else knows?"

"At this point, just Charles and you."

"And does Charles know you've approached me?"

"He does now."

Rick moved his hand to the back of his neck. "And you want me to what? Inform on my colleagues or something like that?"

Now it was Abigail's turn to look surprised. "Is that what you ... oh, for God's sake no," she stammered, quickly recovering and regarding him seriously once more. "Look Professor –"

"Rick," he interjected.

Her face softened slightly. "Fine. Rick. The Medical Examiner and I are awaiting the results from the initial autopsy, and depending on what we learn, I may need to enlist your professional assistance. That's all."

When he could think of nothing more to add, Rick nodded simply and said, "Ok."

Chapter 13

"I think I've got it, Professor."

Rick glanced across the room to the far bench and noticed the student looking at him expectantly. "I'll be right there, Jenny." He finished assisting a young man with his mount technique and walked over to her, pulled up an empty stool beside hers and gestured to the scope.

"May I?"

"This one has much better contrast," she said proudly. "And I was more cautious in the prep after what you said last time about my dilution."

Rick gave her a polite smile and bent down to align the eyepieces to his face. He used his left hand on the knobs to shift the location of the slide. "This is much better. You had so many clustered before it was almost impossible to do a proper count. How many drops of ammonium chloride did you use?"

"One, but I increased the sample volume to eleven milliliters."

"Well, it seems to have worked. You let them dry nicely too. This came from the big shoal sample?" He sat upright and turned his gaze to her.

She beamed at this small accomplishment. "Yes, from the snails we collected a couple days ago."

"By the deadfall?" Rick pictured the old cedar that had been uprooted and fallen into the water sometime within the past few years. Its upper portion lay partially submerged in the shallow sandy water, stripped of branches so that only the trunk remained.

"Yes. Lisa and I collected a few samples from there and did the prep on them."

Rick peered into the scope once more, silently adjusting the fine focus as he scanned the sample. "This is really nice, Jenny. You have a lot of *Argus*." He adjusted the slide once more and sat back. "Take a look at this one next to the pointer."

She peered into the eyepiece and saw roughly a half dozen samples of *Epithemia argus* in various positions, several with striking detail of their fine and course transverse lines along the diatom frustule. One was positioned next to the eyepiece pointer, its wedge shaped body lying in such a way that the valve face was clearly evident. "Ooh, that it a nice one!" she said excitedly, clearly pleased her collection had been so successful.

Rick reached down the table, grasped a small pamphlet, and slid it in front of her. "You're all set now," he said smiling. "Argus is the easy one in that slide, because you have so many. There are several others for you to identify in your preparation." He gestured to her open notebook on the table. "Make sure to record the counts for any species you identify for several fields of view. Don't worry if you're only able to match the genus level and not the species. Some of the diatoms are nearly impossible to identify all the way down."

"And you want us to record the water parameters on the same page in the notebook?"

Rick nodded and pointed to the upper corner of the data page. "Yes, and I suggest you just be consistent when you do more data. So, for this set, put the date, location, water temperature and the other parameters we collected here. We'll do subsequent collections from other sites, and you should record your data in the same way to make it easier to cross compare."

Jenny gave him a silent thumbs up. "Will we collect again from where we were a couple days ago?"

"You mean by the shoal?"

She nodded.

"Yes," Rick replied. "We'll do a couple more collections from that site over the course of the next month. I want you all to see how the species distributions change as the summer unfolds and the water dynamics evolve." With that, he pushed his stool backward and began to stand.

"Professor?" she asked in a tentative voice.

Rick turned toward her, expecting a question having to do with the data. Her expression suggested something else.

"A few of us were wondering why the police were here again yesterday."

Rick thankfully remained impassive. "You mean the patrol car at the administration building?"

"That, and my friend Tyler said he saw all the faculty go into the lecture hall with a uniformed officer." Though she seemed casual in her manner of speaking, Rick detected a slight undertone of innocent concern. "So what's up? Is there something going on we should know about?"

He looked directly into her eyes and allowed a placid expression to play on his face, hoping to convey what he intended. "Nothing to worry about. We had a required staff training session yesterday on sexual harassment."

Her eyes widened slightly at this.

"Like I said, there's nothing to worry about," he added reassuringly. "The State mandates all institutes of higher education comply with regulations about identifying workplace issues, and we were overdue to take the class." He hoped this lie would be enough. "Normally, these kind of things are done on-line and don't require everyone to meet. However, here –"

She smiled knowingly, "I know. Spotty internet coverage."

"That's it," he said simply. "So, nothing to worry about."

#

The noon sun reflected off the gravel along the front drive. Rick lifted his eyes as he walked until his gaze found where the distant road curved along the shore toward the faculty housing, its surface indistinct from rising heat waves. A steady breeze came off the bay to his left, where whitecaps rolled one after another onto the sandy shore, lifting small bits of detritus back and forth along the shallow incline of the beach.

"Hey Professor!" shouted a young man who recognized him as he passed by the old cement slab where the basketball pole was affixed. Two students, both shirtless and in short cutoffs, played a game of one on one, and Rick gave a wave as he walked by.

"Got a moment?" said David, who had suddenly appeared next to him.

Rick jumped. "Jesus, you scared me." He glanced overhead and noticed the wind whipping through the sparse canopy of shoreline trees. "I didn't hear you coming."

David motioned ahead to a small covered gazebo, which contained a couple well-worn picnic tables underneath. A wooden placard on the roofline read 'Chatterbox'. "I need to talk with you for a moment." He fell in beside him as they made their way to the shade beneath the open roof.

Rick used the tabletop as his seat, letting his feet rest on the bench chair below. "It feels like July now, doesn't it?"

David took a seat beside him. "At least there's a breeze here."

"I bet its murder on the upper field."

David cast a sideways glance. "Yeah. It's baking up there right now. Did you mean to say it that way?"

Rick realized his unfortunate choice of words. "Sorry about that. Nothing intended." Rick looked across the road to the Administration Building and saw Heather ascend the cement steps and enter the mailroom. "That reminds me." He turned back to David, who regarded him expectantly. "Did Heather come talk to you?"

"Do you mean about doing a possible research project?"

Rick smiled. "I guess that means she did. Good. She mentioned it to me, and I told her you might be interested." He winced slightly. "I hope that's ok. Are you?"

"What? Interested?"

Rick nodded.

David laughed. "Of course. I mean, Susan and I are a little swamped now with data for the big grant, but it can't hurt to plan ahead."

"From what she described, it doesn't sound like there would need to be many changes to your existing set up."

"Yeah, not really. I imagine with a little funding we could construct some larger units to allow for more diversity in the plants. We're fairly limited right now for my research, and I suspect she'd need a range of pollinators to monitor in the elevated CO_2 environment."

"Well," Rick grinned. "Funding for climate change is a boon, and you'll find Heather is surprisingly persistent."

A white station truck drove slowly by, trailing a cloud of dust behind it, thankfully downwind from where they sat. Rick watched as it receded down the gravel road. "You wanted to talk to me about something?" he said simply.

David's face darkened as he met Rick's eyes. "About Peter. Well, actually about Peter and Elise." He waited to gauge Rick's reaction, and seeing nothing he added, "My place is two down from his."

Rick's eyes narrowed as he tried to imagine where this was headed. "Uh huh."

"It was so damn hot the other night, I couldn't sleep. I got up around two in the morning and got a glass of milk."

Rick's eyebrows lifted at this. "Milk? Tell me you're joking."

"May I continue?" David said, faking indignance. "So, I went out on the back porch to get out of the stifling atmosphere of the cottage, and I had been siting there for several minutes when I heard voices from Peter's place."

"From two cottages down?"

David nodded. "It was completely still out, and their voices carried almost as clearly as if they were sitting next to me."

"Peter and Elise?"

"Yes. Well, mostly Peter. I could just make out what he was saying, and it was something about seeing Sondra on the river a few days ago."

"The day of her disappearance."

"It sounded like it. And I heard Elise say something about telling the police. Then, Peter's voice raised a little, and though it was difficult to hear, he was rather adamant about not saying anything."

"Wait a minute," Rick interjected. "Two nights ago?"

David nodded again.

"So, Peter had seen Sondra on the river on the day of her disappearance, and he failed to say anything when Officer Bennett told us about finding her body?" He shook his head slowly and whispered, "Jesus. What the hell does that mean?"

"I have no idea," said David. "I was hoping you might."

"Why me?" Rick replied incredulously.

"Because, I can't think of anyone else who even tolerates, let alone knows Peter as well as you do."

Rick laughed sarcastically and gave his friend a look of disbelief. "David, you've got it wrong there. Peter's just as arrogant and condescending to me as the rest of us. I have no idea why –"

"Why what?" came Heather's lilting voice unexpectedly as she neared them from the roadside.

David looked up sharply at her approach. "Oh, hi there Heather."

"Why what?" she repeated.

He glanced quickly to Rick, who simply nodded. "I was just telling Rick here about an incident from the other night," he said, after which he repeated the scenario to her astonishment.

Heather looked quickly back and forth between them. "You've got to be kidding me. You think Peter's involved?"

"Involved," Rick parroted. "I think we have to be careful here and not jump to conclusions. It's no secret Peter was antagonistic to Sondra. The timing was tight for him to locate another Monkeyflower. She made it clear she'd be collecting data from the upper branch." He turned to them with a knowing expression. "We have no way of knowing for sure if he even truly found the plant at all."

"One of you should mention this to Officer Bennett," Heather said.

David stood slowly and faced them both. "Probably."

"And you'll speak to her directly when she returns?" Rick said.

David exhaled. "When she returns," he repeated softly as he turned and began walking up the road toward the Grapevine Point shore. "Who would have thought," he said over his should as he departed.

#

"You should tell her," Heather said. When he didn't respond, she added "That's probably why David wanted to speak with you about it in the first place."

"David has no idea of my private discussion with Abigail." He then looked at her meaningfully. "No one is supposed to know about my discussion with her."

"*You* told *me*," she said suggestively.

"And I probably shouldn't have." He saw her feign a hurt expression. "Oh please. I knew you saw me speaking with her, and frankly I didn't want to keep a secret."

"From the camp?" she said innocently.

"From you, of course. And don't pretend you wouldn't try to badger me."

Heather smiled subtly. "Fine." She reached over and placed her hand on his arm. "Have you given more thought to what she said?"

"Of course."

She waited expectantly.

"And, there's only one of two things to conclude. On the one hand, perhaps the police already have reason to suspect that her murder – "

"Assuming it's murder."

"Ok, fair enough – have reason to suspect that Sondra's murder was done by someone inside the camp, and so they may want an inside contact."

Heather shook her head dubiously. "Doesn't seem like the police would operate that way."

"Using inside information?"

"Not in an orchestrated way, no. Besides, how could she even be sure she could trust you?"

"Well then," he said resignedly. "It must be the other reason."

"Which is?" she said expectantly.

"There's obviously a connection between us, and she wants to pursue it," he teased.

Heather deadpanned her response. "Yes, that's it. All this so that Officer Bennett can make advances toward you."

Rick chuckled softly. "Well, I guess I'll find out soon enough."

"Yes, I suppose you will," she replied reflexively, distracted as two students rode past on a pair of old camp bicycles. "Wait! What do you mean by that?"

"I mean she contacted me earlier today, and we've arranged to meet late this afternoon."

"You're serious?"

Rick nodded soberly. "Not a date, I'm afraid." He winced a little saying this and raised his hand apologetically. "Sorry. I shouldn't be joking about it."

"Is she coming here?"

"No. I'm going to Cheboygan at her request. I thought initially it was because the County Station is located there, and while I'm sure that's part of it, I suspect it may also have something to do with the autopsy."

Heather looked at him gravely. "Why the autopsy?"

"Office Bennett mentioned on the phone that she wanted to discuss with me something about the results, which meant I needed to come to Cheboygan."

"Surely, you won't have to –"

Rick shrugged. "I'd rather not think about it, which is why I'm trying to joke about going on a date."

Chapter 14

Abigail held the door and motioned for Rick to enter the small conference room. Inside, an oval table dominated the space, with several folding chairs around the perimeter, including two that were occupied.

"Dr. Parsons," Abigail began formally, "let me introduce Stephen Bishop and Dr. Andrew Riley." Both men stood and extended a hand simultaneously toward Rick as he approached.

"Dr. Parsons," said Stephen as he shook Rick's hand. He was tall and slender, with an angular face highlighted by a hawk-shaped nose and wire-rimmed spectacles and straight salt and pepper hair pulled back neatly into a ponytail.

"I'd prefer Rick, if it's all the same to you."

Stephen nodded cordially and sat down again. "It's Steve."

"And I'm Andy," smiled the second man as he introduced himself. "I performed the autopsy on Dr. Parker." Where Steve was slender to the point of wiry, Andrew was the opposite. He leaned over with a corpulent hand and grasped Rick's firmly. Rick thought he detected a hint of preservative fumes as they greeted one another.

Abigail shut the door behind her and took the nearest seat, placing a large manila folder on the table. "Since we're all informal here, which I think is preferable by the way, Steve is the County Medical Examiner who was on scene with me at Lake Kathleen when the body was recovered. He also serves as a deputy for certain cases."

Rick glanced to both men. "My guess is you already know I'm Rick Parsons from the Biological Station, and I'm a faculty member in plant biology."

"I'm curious about Erasmus," Steve said. "Obviously you go by Rick, but I'm to understand your proper name is –"

"Yes, is Erasmus Parsons," Rick finished reluctantly.

"Family name?" said Andrew.

Rick huffed softly. "You'd think. At least, that might have made things a little more bearable growing up." He glanced from one to the other. "Ever heard of Erasmus Darwin?"

The group looked at one another blankly.

"How about Charles Darwin?"

"Of course," said Abigail, as both Steve and Andy nodded their heads in agreement.

"The short story is Erasmus Darwin was Charles' grandfather, and I, for better or worse, was named after the elder Darwin."

Abigail's face registered bewilderment. "You're saying you were named after Charles Darwin's grandfather?"

"Unfortunately, yes," Rick replied. "My parents were amateur naturalists, particularly my father. He considered himself a 'lover of plants.'" Rick laughed slightly at what was obviously a private joke. "Sorry about that. *Loves of Plants* was a partial title of one of Erasmus Darwin's writings back in the late 1700s, and my folks were so enamored with his prose they decided to name their only son after him."

Steve and Andy looked to one another, not sure how to react. Abigail merely raised her eyebrows.

"And you can see why I tend to go by Rick, rather than Erasmus," he added.

"And you became a plant biologist yourself?" said Andrew.

"Call it coincidence or fate," Rick said. "I stopped wondering myself a long time ago."

Abigail opened the folder before her. "All right then, Rick. You want to know why we've asked you here?"

Again he looked from one face to another. "I suspect you've found something that requires a biological expertise?"

Abigail folded her hands in front of her and nodded. "What do you know about drowning?"

At once, Rick's mind conjured a gruesome image of Sondra's lifeless body floating near the surface of what he could only presume was Lake Kathleen. He blinked several times to clear his thoughts. "I guess I know what the majority do. A person can't breathe. Their lungs fill with water. They asphyxiate. The brain effectively dies from a lack of oxygen." He looked directly at Abigail, "Sondra drowned."

"Yes. Both the circumstantial evidence from the initial crime scene and the findings from Andrew support the conclusion that Dr. Parker died from drowning."

Rick held his hand up and interrupted. "Wait! Wait a minute! You said 'crime scene,' correct? I take it you don't believe Sondra accidentally drowned in Lake Kathleen?"

"No," said Steve. "We don't. Dr. Parker's body was visible on the bottom of the lake from our recovery boat, and that fact alone typically supports an initial supposition of a recent death by drowning."

"I'm not sure I understand," Rick said.

"What Steve means is that a submerged body, particularly one in relatively shallow water, supports an initial hypothesis of a recent drowning, provided the victim wasn't weighted down. When a person's lungs fill with water as they drown, their buoyancy decreases to the point they will actually sink in freshwater. With deep water, a body will lose buoyancy even more, as the pressure of increasing depth compacts any internal body air." Abigail paused and took a sip of coffee. "Ok so far?"

Rick nodded, and she gestured for Steve to continue.

"Upon death, internal decomposition produces respiratory gases that actually bloat the body cavities, typically causing a submerged body to float again. This process is hastened in warmer water, and can occur usually within a couple days. Lake Kathleen is somewhat colder, although not overly so, and since the body was in relatively shallow water, and since our divers found no evidence of her being submerged with weights, we concluded initially the likelihood of drowning."

"All that before recovery?" Rick said incredulously.

Abigail nodded soberly. "You have to understand, Rick, particularly with this type of circumstance, much of how we make a definitive determination requires the recovery team be thorough in evaluating the circumstantial evidence. Despite what the public often believes through television and otherwise, there is no real targeted pathological test to determine if death was indeed caused principally by drowning."

"Can I have a drink of water?" Rick asked almost quietly. He was trying desperately to banish the grotesque images of Sondra's corpse from his imagination. "This is all a little surreal to me. I just spoke with Sondra only several days ago."

Andrew stood up and gave Rick a sympathetic expression. "I'll be right back with a glass."

"I know this is difficult, Rick," Abigail said. "We

apologize for what may appear callousness on our part. Unfortunately, we've experienced this and other rather gruesome scenes as a part of the job."

Rick licked his lips and took several shallow breaths. "Go on."

"When the body was recovered, there were certain other indications that strongly supported the hypothesis of drowning," Steve continued, studying Rick's face to gauge how much more detail was necessary at this point.

"Wait!" Rick suddenly became alert, remembering his earlier question. "Again, you said crime scene. In fact, you said an *initial* crime scene. What does that mean?"

Steve nodded once again. "There was almost no froth cone of any sort around the victim's nose or mouth, nor was there any indication of the presence of vomit traces."

"Which suggests the victim was unconscious prior to being submerged in the water," added Abigail. "A conscious drowning victim expels a mixture of mucous, water and air."

"There are other indicators, such as —" Steve hesitated, seeing Abigail shake her head slightly back and forth.

"I don't think Rick either needs or wants to hear those details."

Steve's lips formed a thin line. "Yeah. Understood." He held Rick's gaze. "You ok?"

"Yes," Rick replied evenly. "Go on."

"While inspecting the victim's skull, I found evidence of a notable contusion on the left parietal bone," Steve curved his right arm up and behind his own head so that his fingers lightly touched a place just to the right and slightly higher than his own left ear. "Beneath her hair was a two centimeter break in the skin, and there were signs of subcutaneous blood pooling."

"Someone hit her?" Rick blurted.

"Yes," said Abigail. "Our initial hypothesis supports Dr. Parker was struck in the back of the head with such severity she lost consciousness. She was then submerged and killed by asphyxiation due to drowning."

Andrew had returned with both a large glass of water and a cup of coffee. Rick thanked him and disregarded the water, needing instead the warmth and clarity the coffee would provide. "And the autopsy?" he directed at Andrew.

"Supports the hypothesis. Let me just say the victim had certain physiological indicators which corroborate the initial findings of a death by drowning, moreover one that took place while the victim was unconscious from a blunt force trauma to the rear of her skull."

Rick sat back and looked from one face to another. "Do you have any leads?"

Abigail shook her head. "We are unable to discuss that with you, Rick." She saw his eyes narrow and his forehead bunch together. "Please understand, our investigation is proceeding accordingly. That said, we simply cannot talk about the particulars of the subsequent investigation with you."

He leaned forward abruptly and placed both hands forcefully palm down on the table. "Then what the hell am I doing here?"

Abigail took another sip from her cup and gestured to Rick that he do the same. "Bear with me for minute."

Rick simply raised his hands in what was a combination of submission and frustration. "I'm listening."

"Rick, though there is much to admire about the level of sophistication of law enforcement and medical forensics in both Emmet and Cheboygan counties, in truth we are still fairly underfunded and frankly a little archaic compared to comparable counties downstate. Typically under these circumstances, I would enlist the help of a colleague who operates out of Traverse City, but unfortunately he has been in a recent accident and is, to but it bluntly, incapacitated."

"What type of colleague do you mean?"

"Well, not to be overly vague, but *your* type of colleague."

Again Rick raised his hand in confused irritation.

"Under certain circumstances, I will utilize the services of forensic specialists to gather and or analyze data regarding a potential crime scene."

The realization suddenly hit him. "You want me to do forensic work."

"I believe you have the requisite experience to assist our investigation, yes."

"But I'm a teacher, for Christ's sake! I'm not a trained forensic scientist." Rick sat back once again, his voice lowering slightly. "I have colleagues in other institutions who are called to testify for certain cases. Several of them even do the forensic work."

Abigail sensed his consideration. "We could help you with the required sample protocol for recording and storage."

"You want me to qualify her algal profile to see if it matches the lake. Is that it?"

"And if so," added Steve, "it may streamline our subsequent investigation."

"Would the Station be aware of my assistance?"

On hearing this question, Abigail gave him a reassuring smile. "The Director would be made aware of your work. And I'd have to confirm you have sufficient resources to secure both the samples we provide and any data you collect."

"Secure?" Rick said curiously. "Why on Earth – "

"For one primary reason," Abigail interrupted. "Though I could conceivably imagine another. Principally, there is the issue of maintaining custody. It is rather critical we establish a strict protocol for the custody of any samples and/or data, so that any legal counsel will consider potential evidence as secure and viable from that perspective."

"Good Lord," Rick whispered almost disbelievingly. "And the other reason?"

"For your protection, and the protection of the evidence, in the event your ongoing forensic work becomes known." She gave him a meaningful look, and he wondered if she was inferring something about Heather.

This time, he reached for the cup of water and drank it quickly, suddenly aware of the sensation of cold liquid pouring down his throat to the extent he sputtered and coughed.

"You ok, Rick?" Abigail said, noticing what looked like a repugnant expression on his face.

Rick placed the cup hesitantly back on the table and used the back of his hand to wipe his mouth. He looked to each of them slowly once more and nodded. "When would I begin?"

#

Heather lifted the empty beer bottle from the red and white gingham tablecloth and held it aloft with a slight shake, catching the eye of the waitress who ambled over to retrieve it from her.

"Can I bring you another?"

She glanced at them expectantly, waiting as Rick stared vacantly for several uncomfortable seconds.

Heather reached over and placed a hand on his arm, jolting him back to the present. "You might as well bring us both another," she said smiling to her.

The waitress leaned in and deftly raised Rick's bottle to see if it was empty. "Looks like you're still working on this, hon. I'll be back shortly with two more." She turned and began to navigate around a nearby table, calling back to them. "Your order will be ready in just a few minutes."

Heather looked at him sarcastically and in a contrived Northern Michigan accent parroted, "Your order should be ready soon, hon," placing notable emphasis on the latter term of endearment.

Rick shrugged. "I can't help it if total strangers call me by sweet nothings."

"I suspect if we eavesdrop closely, we'll hear her call nearly every man in this room hon or honey." Heather's voice had reverted to her normal, soft-spoken Irish accent. She glanced around the darkened room, letting her eyes admire the walls made of varnished logs with white chinking in between, the large stone fireplace in the center of the room, and the open rafters above, adorned with various taxidermies from the north woods. "You said you've been coming here a long time?"

"Every summer my whole life."

"Has it always looked this way?"

Rick looked quickly about the room. "This main room's been about the same ever since, well ... ever since my parents were teenagers when the place first opened." He gestured to the connecting door that led past the fireplace into another room. "I think through there used to be a bar, and it was sunk down a little, like you had to step down to enter it. The outside was also stained dark brown, like it is inside." He shrugged. "I think they switched to that mustardy yellow a few years ago. Still, Vivio's has pretty much been the same my whole life."

Heather took notice of the lingering groups of people still waiting outside the window for an available seat then stole a glance at her phone. "I can't believe there's still a line to get seated. It's after eight o'clock."

"And I still can't believe you haven't been here before."

"That's what one of my students said this afternoon when I told her I was coming here." Heather closed one eye and theatrically pushed her mouth to one side, "How did she put it? Yes, that it was easily the best pizza in the state."

"I'll second that!" Rick said as he leaned back to make room for the server who had returned with two bottles and placed them cautiously among the other items on the table. He waited until she had departed before taking a long, slow drink and turning to meet her eyes. "This was an interesting day. And by the way, thanks for giving me some time to just decompress."

"Do you want to talk about it now?"

"Yes, but I'm not sure how much I can tell you about –"

"That they want you to do some forensic work," Heather interrupted.

Rick's eyes widened, and she laughed softly in seeing this. "How in the hell did you –"

"Lucky guess," she added. "Well, actually that's not entirely true. Out of curiosity I went to the Station Library after you left for Cheboygan. I used the net to do a little research about your Officer Bennett."

Rick wondered if her use of 'your' Officer was a subtle barb, but he decided not to pursue it.

"She has an impressive background. Spent several years downstate working in Ann Arbor. It's a mystery why she'd want to move up here after –"

"Jan said she grew up here," he interrupted, shrugging his shoulders. "Maybe to be closer to family."

"Well, given her impressive background, perhaps its no wonder things have been turned over to Cheboygan."

Again Rick's eyes widened slightly. "You're the clever one."

"Not really. Although, it is curious Emmet County abdicated so quickly." She looked at him inquiringly. "I assume that's the case?"

"Yes, off the record."

"Do they have a suspect?"

Rick shook his head. "They wouldn't discuss it with me."

"Ahh," Heather said. "Of course. This makes sense if you've been asked to assist them. Your Officer Bennett-"

Rick's voice rose slightly. "How come you keep saying it like that?"

"Saying what?"

"*Your* Office Bennett."

Heather eyed him mischievously. "Just to tease you a little."

"Well, I think you can drop the *your* thing."

"Fine," she demurred. "At any rate, Officer Bennett has been consulted on several regional homicides. I read several reports where she was called in to assist the lead detectives on evidence collection. Evidently, she's fairly progressive with forensic analyses."

Rick took another long draw of beer and set the empty bottle back on the table. "Now I get it. Fine. At least this way I can honestly claim I didn't tell you anything." He continued to stare absently at the bottle.

"What is it?" said Heather.

He met her eyes with a hint of a smile. "Just thinking about what *my* Officer Bennett said earlier about taking precautions for my security."

"Let me guess," Heather said, reaching across the table to take his hand in hers. "Should it become known you are doing forensic work, you might be put in danger."

He liked the feel of her hand in his. "Something like that." He laughed then. "I have a feeling she was referring to you."

"That I am dangerous?"

"No, not that, of course. I think she was signaling to me that I have to keep things confidential even from you."

"How would she even know we -" Heather started and then trailed off, slightly shy at declaring things.

Rick sensed her vulnerability. "Oh *my* Officer Bennett has a strong intuition about me." He gave her a sly grin. "That, or it's more likely she asked Peg or Jan."

"Ah," Heather said softly. "That may be a little difficult now."

"No one else knew I went to Cheboygan?"

"You mean except Charles and me." Heather replied.

"That's right."

She shook her slowly. "As far as I know, the answer is no."

He squeezed her hand as the waitress returned with a large tray of pizza. "Then let's see what happens next."

#

Rick pulled out of the parking lot and steered the car into the left turn lane.

Heather gave him a curious look. "Why are we going this way?" She glanced through the windshield across toward the far woods, seeing the rustic entrance sign for the Cross In the Woods. "Don't tell me you're taking me –"

He accelerated into the intersection and steered the car left onto the county road traveling west. "No, I'm not taking you to the Cross!" Rick's eyes followed the entrance as it passed by on their right. "Though you ought to go see it for yourself. It's pretty amazing."

"Isn't it just a big crucifix in the woods?" Heather's mind conjured images of Midwest sideshow attractions, like the giant ball of string or the largest collection of dinosaur coprolites. She looked at him dubiously.

Rick laughed. "Ok, yes. It's just a big cross in the woods, but I have to admit it's pretty cool. You walk a bit from the parking lot through the trees, and then all of a sudden this giant redwood crucifix commands the clearing."

"If you say so," Heather replied, letting her eyes settle on the road ahead. "Well if that's not the reason for going this way, what is?"

Rick gestured ahead. "I wanted to see something up here where the road curves."

They drove silently for a couple miles, occasionally catching glimpses of the blue water of Burt Lake through the thick trees on the right as the road began to ascend a gentle hill. Rick slowed as they reached the crest and pointed suddenly to the right shoulder, where the guardrail ended and a small access road led off into the woods. In the grassy berm on the far side stood a large oak, its front face scarred by what must have been a recent impact. "See that tree?" Rick turned into the access road and brought the car to a stop. They both noticed what appeared to be skid marks in the grass leading to the trunk.

"What happened here?"

"This is where Mike Pritchard had an accident."

Heather looked at him with surprise.

"Peg told me the other day he was involved in a car crash here." He noticed a strange expression on her face. "I guess I forgot to tell you with all the other stuff that's taken place."

"How did it happen?"

Rich shrugged as he examined the tire marks through the grass. "Peg said he lost control. His airbags deployed, and I guess he hit his head in the impact."

Heather was looking out her window back down the road in the direction from the direction they'd just come. There aren't any marks on the road back that way. There's nothing on the access either." She turned back to him. "It looks like he just decided to drift right from the main road and straight toward the tree."

"That's exactly what I was thinking."

"Did he see a deer or something?" she said.

Rick shook his head. "I don't know. Peg didn't say." He turned his head to look back over his shoulder through the rear windshield. "Is there anyone coming your way? I can't see."

"You're all clear."

Rick put the car in reverse and did a quick three-point turn, hesitating before steering back onto the county road. "What do you think?"

"Are you asking me if I think it's a bit strange he had an accident at nearly the same time things were taking place on Lake Kathleen?"

Rick raised his eyebrows. "I said before you're the clever girl."

"I don't know what to make of it, really," she replied. "But I bet *your* Officer Bennett may be wondering the same sort of question."

Rick sighed and pulled out into the road toward Alanson. "There you go again."

Chapter 15

"Should I retain the services of private counsel?"

Abigail struggled to keep her face composed, despite her inner conflict whether she'd rather strangle Peter or outright laugh at him for using such pompous language. Instead, she took a deep breath and glanced out the lab window, giving the impression his question deserved careful thought.

"Of course, you are within your right to have an attorney present," she replied, turning back to him with an expression she hoped was passive. "I want to stress again I am only conducting a preliminary series of questions with all faculty and staff here at the station. I have already spoken with several of your colleagues, and none of them thought it necessary to hire counsel. You do, however, have the option to do so." Abigail hoped this deception would suffice.

Peter drummed his fingers softly on the smooth lab bench and regarded her with mild disdain. "I suppose there is no harm in speaking with you, for I have nothing to do with Dr. Parker's disappearance."

"You mean death, Dr. Cummings."

Peter flinched slightly while at the same time his fingers became still. "Yes, of course. Of course that's what I meant."

Abigail placed an open folder on the bench and removed a sheet of paper, sliding it over to him. It contained a topographical map of the East Branch of the Maple River, beginning from its origin at Douglas Lake and winding downstream toward its terminus at Lake Kathleen. She watched Peter's eyes narrow as he scanned the image.

"Show me on this map exactly where your research site is located."

Peter's looked up quickly. "Why?"

Rather than answer directly, Abigail reached over and indicated a general spot on the southern portion of Lake Kathleen. "Dr. Parker's body was found in this vicinity." She traced her finger slowly up the curving line of the East Branch, pausing when she came to the dotted line that marked the location of the access road. "I'm to understand you park the station truck here, is that correct?"

"Yes." He leaned in and pointed to a place upstream where the river entered into a shaded green portion of the map. "This section marks the boundary of the Station Property. There's a rough trail that goes from the pull out where I leave the truck into the woods for several hundred yards. It eventually comes near enough to the river here," he indicated at a spot where the blue line began turning northward toward Robinson Road. "That's my research site."

Abigail studied the map a few seconds longer then turned her attention to him. "The night of Dr. Parker's presentation, you said something about the Monkeyflower."

Peter shifted his finger to where the dam was indicated at the southern end of Lake Kathleen. "That's correct. There's a flowering patch of Monkeyflower here below the dam, and as I stated the other evening, it is the only known local grouping of this endangered species to produce viable pollen."

"And you believe the dam removal would jeopardize this fact?"

His voice rose slightly. "Monkeyflower grows under very unusual conditions. It requires moist and slightly acidic soil, and for reasons we don't really understand, of the very few known groups only the one below the dam is viable. So, if you are asking me if I think the removal of the dam is a likely risk to this particular site, my answer is adamantly yes."

Abigail began to ask a follow-up question but was cut short. "There is no way the DNR can effectively claim the hydrological conditions near the existing site will be unaffected by what is essentially a massive disruption to the existing flow. What I can guarantee is that the surrounding area will be denuded of vegetation as the workers begin to lower the embankment after the diverters have lowered the lake. This site will be drastically changed regardless of whatever safeguards they claim to put in place beforehand."

"What about the Monkeyflower you discovered at your site?"

Peter regarded her with a new appreciation. "I see you were paying attention that evening."

"I believe you said something about its reproductive status?"

"The patch is located on a soft berm next to the river in a spot that contains several tussocks."

"Tussocks?"

"Raised grassy patches. They thrive in the sunny spots along portions of the river bank where the water rarely gets high enough to cover them and yet they're close enough to the water beneath the soil to allow certain plants to thrive. The Monkeyflower there has flowers. Brilliant yellow flowers. I was checking them the day I heard Sondra – " He stopped short, too late.

165

Abigail pretended not to hear him clearly. "And do you have any idea where Dr. Parker was doing temperature measurements?" For a moment, she considered adding the words "on the day she disappeared," but decided instead to see how much he would reveal.

Peter's face twitched slightly as he thought she'd not heard him. "It depends where Dr. Parker started." He pointed once again to the map, indicating the northeast corner of the lake where the East Branch emptied. "It's almost a mile and half from the lake up to where the river crosses underneath Robinson Road. Then another mile or so through the Station forest to Douglas Lake Road, and maybe a mile as it winds again until the origin at Douglas. I suspect she would have wanted to do baseline measurements every thousand feet, which means roughly between five and seven locations in each of the sections of the river. It's not easy going anywhere above Lake Kathleen, mostly because there are few access points, and the Maple gets narrower the further up you go toward Douglas. It's full of deadfalls and overhanging vegetation in places." Peter's eyes narrowed as he did a quick mental calculation. "My guess it would have taken her nearly a week to get things done."

"Where would you have started, were you in her place?"

His mind quickly decided on the proper answer to lessen her suspicion. "I would have begun at Douglas and gone downstream, mostly to get the difficult sections out of the way first."

"Which means she was likely here," she pointed to the deep woods between Douglas Lake Road and Van Road, "around the time of her disappearance."

Peter nodded slightly. "That seems reasonable enough."

Abigail quickly decided to change the subject to

gauge his reaction. "Isn't it the case your research funding is heavily contingent on your site along the branch?"

"I don't see what this has to – "

"And correct me if I'm wrong," she continued, "but your doctoral student, what is her name?"

Peter glared at her and said nothing.

"Dr. Cummings?"

"Elise. Her name is Elise Mathers."

"Ah, that's it. Thank you, I had forgotten. And your Ms. Mathers, I presume her own doctoral research dovetails with your own."

Peter's voice turned icy as he crossed his arms in front of him, regarding her with renewed contempt. "Officer Bennett. I demand to know what it is you are implying with these new questions."

Abigail remained perfectly neutral. "It's nothing to worry about, Dr. Cummings. At this point, I'm simply trying to get an overall picture of the characters who are most closely associated with the work on the river. It is the case, is it not, if the dam is removed and the Maple River is restored to its natural flow, it may impact your own research site upstream?"

"I believe you already know my feelings on this matter, given your astute observations from the other evening."

"And your hope is the new Monkeyflower will produce viable pollen so the DNR will be forced to reconsider their position on the restoration?"

Peter remained silent.

"Which means, Dr. Cummings, the stakes are fairly high for you. Isn't that the case?"

"I have nothing more to say," he said venomously.

"Then let me leave you with one thing, and you needn't bother to reply at this time. Perhaps another." Abigail looked directly into his face, matching his aggressive expression. "I'm to understand your graduate student has been isolated on the West Branch, far away from your hopeful work at your site. Presumably, she would be the only person to validate or corroborate if indeed any pollen you discover from this new plant actually came from the plant itself and not from, let's say, the existing site below the dam." Abigail watched as Peter's lips tightened. "Is there anything else you want to tell me at this time that may assist with my investigation into Dr. Parker's disappearance and murder?"

With that, Peter quickly stood and began walking toward the door. "I have nothing further to say."

Abigail watched him depart. "For now, Dr. Cummings."

#

Rick held the refrigerator door open and stared fixedly at the four glass bottles Abigail had dropped off for him over an hour ago prior to her meetings. Charles had accompanied her to the lab to serve as a formal witness for the purposes of documenting custody of Sondra's tissue samples. He stood stoically by her side and observed as she placed the small padded cooler on the lab bench and unzipped its lid, removing each bottle carefully to the bench top.

"This is a sample of the victim's lower lung tissue," she stated flatly, nodding to Charles as a reminder he make a notation in the document she gave him prior to their arrival. "Charles, make sure to initial your witness to the transfer in the space next to the description."

Charles merely nodded as his eyes glanced briefly to the pinkish blob inside the jar, which was labeled in bold-faced lettering, 'Parker, Distal Lung.' Each jar was squat and approximately four inches high, with a wide-mouthed opening sealed by an orange twist top cap. He swallowed audibly and took a deep breath, placing the record sheet on a space next to the cooler.

Rick wondered if her use of the word 'victim' was intended to minimize any personal connection for them. He too took a furtive peek at the jar's contents and tried desperately to banish the thought that it was not too long ago within a living and breathing Sondra Parsons.

"You ok so far?" Abigail eyed him warily.

Rick gave her a cursory nod. "Yes."

She extracted the second jar. "Spleen," and then she removed another. "Marrow. Left Femur." Finally, she withdrew a jar that contained only a slightly cloudy liquid. "This is the sample of Lake Kathleen, near where the victim was discovered."

Charles dutifully initialed in the correct spaces then handed the pen to Rick with a meaningful expression. "You're supposed to initial here you've received them."

"Remember," Abigail added. "You need to keep these tissue samples in a locked refrigerator unless you are using one or more of them during your work. Also, I strongly recommend you isolate all equipment you use and any data you generate. Keep your notes secure, and make sure you follow an explicit protocol for analysis." She watched as he gathered all four jars and took them over to one of the lab refrigerators.

"Like I said before, we don't have a locked frig here on campus." He opened the refrigerator door and placed the jars gingerly on the dedicated shelf. "But if you're ok with what I described," Rick added as he closed the door. He then reached for a heavy duty cable with a padlock sitting on a nearby stroller cart. "I'll wrap this around the frig and put the cable through the handle. There's no way, apart from using some beefy cutters, anyone will be able to gain access to the samples without the code."

Abigail nodded her approval. "That will be fine." She then took the custody sheet from Charles and placed her signature in the proper location to signify the release. "They're all yours now, Rick. How long do you think you'll need?"

Rick looked absently at the refrigerator. "Couple of days. There are some additional prep steps I'll need to do to wash the organic component, and I want to be extra careful with the drying time." He turned toward her again. "Expect something by as early as tomorrow evening, but I'll send you an update regardless."

Abigail nodded again and signaled to Charles that they depart, leaving Rick alone to complete his work.

#

"Well?"

"It was actually pretty straightforward," Rick said, looking up from his notebook when he heard Heather approach. "I cleaned each sample with a little deionized water and then prepped them for analysis."

"Heated with nitric acid?" Heather asked, which caused Rick's eyebrows to rise a little. "Don't be so surprised. I did a little reading myself."

"The one with the proteinase step?"

She nodded.

"That's it. I added these in a Tris buffer after doing the centrifuge for seven minutes. Then I did a microfiltration with cellulose and transferred the sediment into some distilled water. I cleaned the organic components with hydrogen peroxide and potassium dichromate and poured off the supernatant."

"How long did that take?"

"About twelve hours, then a little cleaning with deionized. I put samples in coverslips, and they spent some time in the dryer." He gestured to microscope. "I'm nearly finished with the counts."

Heather glanced down at his open notebook. "Bone Marrow?"

"That was my initial reaction when Abigail gave me that sample. As I discovered when I was doing a little reading myself, a drowning victim will ultimately take in water into the upper airway and then to the peripheral lung. There's so much volume it actually makes its way into the pulmonary alveoli and to the pulmonary vein."

Heather appeared as if she'd swallowed something awful. "And to the rest of the body?"

"Often, yes, if the conditions are right. The victim's heart will continue to beat long enough while water is inhaled that it actually travels to the spleen and even the bone marrow."

"But why is it even necessary to get the marrow?"

"It's best to examine the bone marrow from an intact femur, because it's sealed from possible contamination from some external source."

Heather gestured to a slide still located on the phase contrast microscope nearby. "And that?"

"Is a sample from Lake Kathleen. It didn't need as much prep work, since there was no," he paused, searching for a delicate way to say it.

"I got it," Heather said simply. "May I take a look?"

Rick held his hand out toward the scope. "Be my guest."

She positioned herself and adjusted the eyepieces, then spent nearly a half a minute silently scanning the surface of the slide. "This is a nice assemblage. About half are still alive."

"At least the frustules show pigmentation for those, which is a little surprising. The prep should have cleaned them of their pigments. The remainder are just skeletons."

She examined the slide for another fifteen seconds then turned her head toward him. "You've done a count?"

"Yes." He pointed to the notebook by the cube. "I did some quantitative work on several fields."

Heather looked at him impatiently.

"I used the same protocol for the tissue samples, three hundred individuals per slide, which should be enough for significance."

"And?" she said, her voice rising slightly.

Rick gestured loosely to the Kathleen slides. "The algal assemblage of Lake Kathleen is fairly diverse, which makes sense. I mean, the water's relatively warm, and it's getting near July. There's an abundance of *Gomphonema* and *Fragilaria,* along with a fair number of *Aulacoseria*. I have many down to the species identification, but really at this point that level of detail isn't necessary."

"What about the tissues?"

Rick inhaled slowly and brought his hand across the stubble of beard on his chin. "They all show diatom infiltrates, which supports the drowning conclusion."

"So that's it then," she said.

Rick shook his head slowly. "There's more." He gestured again to his handwritten tables within the open notebook. "The tissues had very little *Gomphonema*, and almost no *Fragilaria*. They did have high levels of *Cocconeis* and moderate numbers of *Argus*."

"*Argus*? You mean the Argus I sometimes hear your students talking about?"

"Yes. I have them sample the snails around Douglas, because they're fairly easy to collect and prep as a first go with doing identification."

A realization suddenly occurred to her, and she instinctively put her hand on his arm. "She was in Douglas?"

Again he shook his head slowly. "No. At least, I'm fairly sure she wasn't." He reached over and grabbed what appeared to be a research paper resting partially underneath the notebook. "Couple years ago a student and I did a quick count of some samples. We were interested in how the assemblages changed as the summer unfolded." He silently brought the title page up for her to see.

"Diatom Stratification on the East Branch of the Maple River," she whispered softly then looked sharply to his face. "Where did you do the measurement?"

"We accessed the branch at the easiest place beneath Robinson Road." He looked at her meaningfully. "On the two track."

"Did you take June collections?" she whispered, searching his eyes.

"Yes."

"And you found *Cocconeis* and *Argus* in the Branch."

"At nearly the exact same proportions." His eyes met hers. "The data from two years ago is almost a perfect match for Sondra's tissues."

"Oh my God," Heather said softly. "You don't think —"

Rick held up a hand to silence her as he reached with the other into his front pocket. He removed his cell phone and placed it on the table next to the folder. "I know what you were about to say." He shook his head slowly. "We both know he's a pompous ass, but *this*?"

Chapter 16

Abigail slowed the cruiser as thick woods on either side of State Road gave way to partial clearing. Steve pointed to a gravel drive, fronted by a dilapidated mailbox angled carelessly on a dry rotted post. They pulled to a stop and looked over toward the small house set back a hundred yards in what was essentially a cut field of wild grasses and clover. A separate two-door garage sat next to the house, both doors open with one bay empty, and the other filled with various pieces of what looked from a distance like fishing gear.

Abigail steered the cruiser into the drive and pulled slowly to a stop.

"This is the main office of Maple River Outfitters?" Steve said sarcastically.

She turned the key and unfastened her seatbelt. "What did you expect?"

He allowed his eyes to survey the property. "I guess a little more Harbor Springs than this."

She huffed softly and gestured with a hand in the direction from which they'd just come. "Harbor Springs is that way. And yes, this is technically in the town limits, but the locals lead a little different life than what the summer residents enjoy." She turned her head again toward the house. "Many of them scrape out a living like this and do fairly well, despite the vagaries of having to live in association with the super wealthy."

Steve suspected he'd touched a nerve and said nothing. She looked over at him, sensing his faux pas. "I grew up not far from Cheboygan down near Mullet Lake. We had a similar existence when the summer people arrived, though not to the same degree as here." She reached for the handle and opened the door, pausing briefly as she stood when her cell phone chimed. "This is Bennett," she said.

Steve had exited the cruiser and stood waiting for her by a small walkway that led to the side entrance.

Abigail listened intently for nearly half a minute before responding. "Understood. So all the samples reflect the Branch?" Silence again as she concentrated. "How soon until you finish your analysis?" Abigail glanced at her watch. "Understood. We'll want to meet with you this afternoon, if possible. Thanks for the update, Rick."

Steve eyed her expectantly as she disconnected the cell. "Good news?"

"Later," she commanded, joining him near the walkway. "I'll fill you in after this."

He nodded and gestured toward the side door. Abigail took the lead and approached the entrance, stopping to open a worn screen and knocking firmly on the vinyl side door. "Mike Pritchard," she said loudly. "This is Office Bennett of the Cheboygan Police Department. We'd like to speak with you, please."

Several seconds passed until the pair was startled by the noise of someone moving about in the detached garage. Steve tugged on her sleeve and pointed toward the bay containing the piles of gear, where a man emerged and stood facing them.

"What do you want?" he stated unkindly.

"Mike Pritchard?" she asked firmly, hardly recognizing from the man she admonished the night of the Alliance presentation.

"That's me."

Abigail bypassed Steve and walked slowly back down the walkway, keeping a cautious eye on the man who stood before them. He was dressed in dirty, loose fitting jeans and a similarly soiled khaki work shirt. His left arm was folded across his chest in a blue sling, and his forehead was bandaged.

"Mr. Pritchard, I'm Officer Bennett from the Cheboygan Police Department."

"What's this all about?" he replied, eyeing them carefully as Steve moved to join her, and the trio stood a dozen paces apart.

Abigail nodded to his arm. "I understand you've recently been in an accident."

His eyes narrowed. "In Indian River." He quickly glanced at Steve. "If I remember correctly, that's over twenty miles from Cheboygan."

The significance of this statement wasn't lost on her. "I am aware of that, Mr. Pritchard." She tilted her head subtlety in Steve's direction. "This is my colleague Stephen Bishop."

Mike made no attempt at a greeting but rather continued to stare evenly at her. "What do you want?"

"Mr. Pritchard, are you aware that the Alliance researcher, Dr. Sondra Parker was recently found dead in Lake Kathleen?"

Mike's face remained perfectly expressionless. "I heard about it. It's a real tragedy."

Abigail ignored his lack of sincerity. "Yesterday, my colleague and I went out to the east branch of the Maple River. I presume you are quite familiar with the Branch, given your statements the other evening at the Alliance presentation?"

Mike's eyes widened slightly. "Am I being accused of something here, Officer?"

"Not at all, Sir," she said calmly, hoping a neutral tone would serve to keep him talking. "We're just trying to contact anyone who may have seen or heard something along the river that may assist us with the investigation. Are you willing to help us?"

He regarded them silently for nearly ten seconds before nodding curtly once.

"Thank you. As I said, we've been out on several roads that access both Lake Kathleen and portions of the Branch, trying to find anything useful."

"That Bug Camp scientist works on the middle part of the branch," he offered evenly.

"And we've spoken to him already, but thank you for suggesting it." She looked over his shoulder to the gear stored in the garage behind him. "Been out with clients on the lake or the branch recently?"

He laughed bitterly and pointed with his right hand to the sling. "Not since this happened."

"Of course, that makes sense," Abigail replied neutrally. "Still, when was the last time you were on the river?"

"Just over a week ago. Why?"

"And when did you have the accident?"

His eyes narrowed again. "Then."

"You're saying you were on the branch a week ago the same day you had the accident."

"That's correct."

"Was anyone with you that day? A client maybe?"

"No. I went alone to clear some new deadfalls from a place near one of the deep holes."

"And then you came out and went down to Indian River."

"More or less," said Mike. "I went to meet a friend for dinner who was driving up on 75 to the U.P."

"So you ate dinner, and then?"

"And then I came back home along the Alanson Road. It was late, and I was tired, and I must have dozed off. Next thing I know I swiped into a tree."

"You were able to drive home?"

"I did."

"In your?"

"Truck. My work truck."

"Which is where now?"

"A friend of mine runs a shop in Alanson. Drove it in to get it fixed."

"You didn't inform Indian River?" Mike looked on silently. Abigail gestured to his bandages. "Where'd you get looked at?"

"Petoskey. Had a buddy drive me down a few days later." He saw the questioning look on her face. "I had a good cut on my forehead and my shoulder was dislocated. I didn't think it was all that bad after the accident, but after a couple of days it looked, well -"

"Were you drinking that night?"

Mike stared at her mutely.

"And this was roughly a week ago?"

"That's what I said."

Abigail nodded as if there wasn't much more to say. "Well, I assume you don't have any more information to share."

Mike relaxed slightly, sensing from her tone the exchange was coming to a close. "I rarely see anyone when I'm on the river, except for my clients, of course."

"You ever run into the Station scientist you mentioned?" Abigail hoped this question sounded innocent.

He regarded her evenly again. "I believe that stretch of river is off limits to the public, isn't it?"

"That's right," she replied. "That it is. I suppose you wouldn't exactly cross paths then."

When he didn't reply, Abigail turned to Steve and motioned her head toward the cruiser. "Well, I guess there's not much more to discuss here then. Anything Steve?"

He looked over to the open garage. "I like to do a little fly fishing every once in a while." He pointed toward the gear stored on shelving against the wall and a pair of hip waders hung loosely from a large peg. "Mind if I take a look?"

"You want to look at my gear?"

"Just the waders. I always wanted a pair." He walked over and began to inspect the felt bottoms, leaving Mike and Abigail alone in the middle of the driveway. "These things really help you grip?" he said holding one of the boots upright so the bottom faced them both directly.

"On rocks, yes," Mike said absently, his attention still focused on Abigail.

"Thank you again for speaking with us," she said, distracting him momentarily as Steve rejoined them.

"That's a nice set up you have in there," said Steve, who extended a hand in thanks and nodded as he made his way to the car.

Abigail also extended a hand. "Well, let's hope you're back in business soon." She started toward the cruiser and turned back to him. "If you think of anything further that may assist us with the investigation, please don't hesitate to contact me." With that, she made her way to the car, started the engine and backed out of the driveway onto State Road.

She waited until they had driven a mile up the road and had taken the next right turn toward the direction of the Biological Station. "Did you get it?"

He turned toward her and used his right hand to remove a piece of white cloth from his shirt pocket. "Yeah, I got it."

"That was smoothly done."

"Thanks, Abby." He reached behind him to get a plastic zip lock bag from a container on the back seat and carefully inserted the cloth into it. "I palmed it when I pretended to admire the boots."

"Did you get the felt too?"

"I got it." He suddenly remembered her phone conversation. "Was that Parsons on the phone?"

"Yes. He finished the analysis of the tissue samples."

"Is that why we're going back to the station?"

The road curved through a section of old growth woods, distinguished by even rows of precisely spaced spruce trees on either side, reaching upward nearly eight feet overhead. They passed a rustic sign by the side, which indicated the tract as having been planted by the CCC in the 1930s. "Rick said the algae profile didn't match Lake Kathleen. He's positive she drowned in the east branch."

"The water's that much different?"

"Evidently. He said it's conclusive."

Steve whistled softly and stared idly at the zip lock bag in his lap. "So, she got hit in the head, drowned in the east branch, and then taken to Lake Kathleen."

"It would appear so."

"What did you think of Pritchard?"

She regarded him with a serious expression. "I already spoke with the ER physician who attended him."

He gave her a sly grin. "You've been busy."

"Pritchard showed up the day after Dr. Parker disappeared. He told the physician he'd had an accident a few days before and had waited to get checked out."

"Which is what he said to us."

"But the doc said his contusion was too recent. He said it must have happened within twenty four hours, given its appearance and the way it was beginning to heal."

"So why the charade?"

"Maybe to make it appear his truck couldn't have possibly been on the river during the time of her murder."

Steve shook his head in confusion.

"Something doesn't match, which is why we need to look at that truck."

"In Alanson."

"Yeah. It's on the way."

#

Abigail nearly tripped over a pair of legs which stuck out from underneath the rear section of a late model Jeep.

"I'll be with you in a minute," came a raspy voice, followed by several seconds of strained grunts as something was being wrenched from below. A dirty hand suddenly shot out palm upward, its fingers making a beckoning motion. "There should be a can of Lock Blaster on the bench right there. You mind grabbing it for me and handing it to me?"

Abigail retrieved the spray and placed it squarely into his wriggling hand. "When you're finished, I'd like a word with you, if you don't mind."

The hand retreated underneath. "Yeah, well, you can see I'm a little busy here at the moment. Maybe you could come back in about an hour or –"

She walked purposefully around the side of the Jeep, letting her black work shoes clack loudly on the dirty cement floor. Abigail stopped at where she thought his head might look directly over to her position and said in a calm, firm voice, "I'm Officer Bennett from the Cheboygan Police Department. I'd appreciate your cooperation now, if you don't mind."

Immediately there was the sound of tools being

deposited on the cement, followed by a grating noise as the man shimmied the rolling backboard out in the direction of the rear bumper. Steve stood in the open doorway that led to the attached garage entrance and observed as dirty legs gave way to the settled paunch and disheveled work shirt of a man who struggled to sit up.

He rose ungracefully and regarded them both from a pair of tired-looking eyes set within a face that strangely reminded Abigail of a bloodhound. He turned to face Steve, presuming he was the authority in charge. "Is there a problem?"

"Sorry to bother you like this," Abigail interrupted as she closed the distance between them. "Are you the owner of this shop?"

"Owner. Mechanic. Accountant. Customer Service," he replied gruffly. "What's this about?"

She gestured toward the rear of the garage. "I took the liberty of looking at your inventory out back and around the side."

"Yeah?"

"I expected to find a blue, Ford F-250 here from an acquaintance of yours, I believe. Mr. Michael Pritchard."

A look of bewilderment formed on his face. "I don't know what the hell you're talking about."

"Mr.?"

"Givens," he replied succinctly.

"Is this the only garage in Alanson?" said Steve.

The mechanic regarded him as if he hadn't understood the question.

"Mr. Givens," pressed Abigail. "We're looking for a Ford Pickup that we're to understand had been delivered to a garage in Alanson. We naturally presumed this meant your garage, since you appear to be the only game in town. This truck would have had some extensive damage on the passenger's side from an accident involving a tree. Does any of this ring a bell?"

His attention shifted from Steve, and he chuffed sarcastically. "Most of the cars out back have been here for a long time. People either can't pay or don't care. Either way, I don't exactly have much turnover that I'd lose track of, what did you say? A blue pickup with quarter damage."

"And you've never heard of the name Michael Pritchard?"

He laughed meanly. "Oh, I didn't say that. I know Pritchard."

"Care to elaborate?" said Abigail.

"It's nothing more than past scuffles. We had words. It escalated, that's all."

"You mean here?" said Steve.

Givens regarded him again. "Hell no. Up at Clyde's, couple years back." He laughed meanly again. "Your Pritchard is known for bad drinking and even worse fighting."

"Ahh," Abigail replied, knowingly. "Has a bit of a reputation?"

"You might say that. He gets a little protective about what he considers his own private fishing area."

"You fish?" said Steve.

"I'll put a boat in on Kathleen occasionally, and sometimes get up into the wide part of the branch on the northeast side." He glanced conspiratorially at Abigail. "Stumbled upon him once in the branch with some client. Didn't think much of it until he turned up later at Clyde's. You see my point?"

Abigail extended her hand, signaling the conversation was over. "Sorry to have bothered you, Mr. Givens."

He started to return the gesture then stopped short when he noticed his greasy palm. "I'm not sure you want to –"

She grasped firmly. "No problem, Mr. Givens. Again, we're sorry to have interrupted your work." She released his hand and began walking toward the entrance door. "By the way, if you hear of anyone doing body work on a Blue F-250, I'd appreciate your giving me a call."

#

"What was that about?"

They had come to the section of 31 heading north where the road widened into a passing lane. Abigail veered the cruiser to the right and glanced in the rearview mirror to see if anyone behind them had the nerve to go by on the left.

"I decided to catch flies with honey, that's all."

Steve's attention was fixed on the approaching sign for the Lake Site Inn on the right, where Woodland Road cut past the restaurant before descending a small hill toward the dam below. He shuddered as he remembered the submerged corpse of Sondra Parker they retrieved only a few days ago. "I imagine it'll be bad enough for the Lake Site when the view's gone. News of the drowning won't help either."

Abigail turned her head quickly, just catching a glimpse of the blue exterior of the restaurant in the distance before a copse of trees passed in front. "Two things," she replied. "First, try to remember where our empathy should lie foremost."

"Yeah, sorry about that," he realized.

"And second, although I don't think it will soften things much, eventually the news will reveal the drowning happened in the branch, if what Rick determined is conclusive."

"What did you say before about honey?"

Abigail chuffed once. "I suspect the repair

community up here in Emmet is fairly fraternal."

"Translate, please."

At that moment, her cell phone began to ring, and Abigail pushed the connect button. "This is Bennett."

The graveled voice of David Givens came through the car's speaker. "Yeah, Officer Bennett, this is Dave Givens. We just spoke fifteen minutes ago in my shop."

"Go ahead Mr. Givens."

"That Blue F-250, the one you were speaking about."

"I'm listening."

"I put a call in to a couple people I know who do private body work. Anyway, I just thought you'd want to know. That F-250 is sitting in a pole barn a half mile up Brutus Road from 31."

"You're certain of this?"

"No, Ma'am. I'm not. But the guy I know is pretty reliable."

Abigail looked over to Steve and saw him nod once. "Ok, Mr. Givens. I appreciate your help." She disconnected the cell and slowed as they approached the outskirts of Pellston. "Flies with honey."

"So Pritchard deliberately lied," Steve said as she pulled the cruiser in a U-turn and headed south on 31.

Abigail nodded. "Again, it would appear so."

"And again, why?"

She pointed ahead through the windshield. "Maybe this time, well learn something."

Fifteen minutes later, she pulled to a stop on the north side of the road. "That must be the pole barn," she said pointing to relatively modern aluminum sided structure next to a small trailer house.

Steve cast his eyes about the property as she steered the car into the grassy two-track from the road. "It doesn't look like anyone's here."

"Best check the front door. I'll go knock while you go take a peek by the barn."

Steve stood from the passenger's side and watched her approached the trailer, thinking for a moment he might accompany her in case of trouble. "You need any –"

"Nope," she said dismissively. "I'll just see if anyone's here. You go on, and be careful. I'll join you in a moment."

He nodded and walked cautiously across the weedy yard to the barn entrance. Two large sliding doors allowed access for vehicles and other big equipment. Steve tried yanking on one and discovered the oversized padlock preventing them from being separated. He walked around the side farthest from the road and came to a regular access door with a glass window embedded in the upper half, the view obscured by a sheet of translucent film. He tried jiggling the handle and found it locked.

By then, Abigail had rejoined him.

"No luck?" she said.

Steve shook his head.

"Possible spare," she said, pointing to the crude wooden platform that served as a step upward into the doorframe.

Steve stepped off, bent down, and lifted the long edge of the platform. "Nothing."

Abigail glanced upward to a light fixture next to the entrance. "Maybe," she said, wriggling her hand inside the frosted white glass bulb. She removed it and proudly held a single key. "How's that for Karma?"

He took it from her and used it to unlock to handle, and they both stepped inside. The ceiling was made of frosted plastic, which allowed enough ambient light to reach the interior so that they didn't need to use the hanging banks of fluorescent bulbs.

Situated in the middle of the floor was the

damaged F-250.

"And there you go," Steve said quietly as he walked slowly around its exterior.

Abigail paused near the front right quarter panel, inspecting the damage to the right side. "How the hell do you get a side impact like this against a tree?" she said softly. "Remind me we need to go to Indian River to do a look at the road where he supposedly went off."

"You should come see this," Steve said calmly from near the rear.

Abigail looked up and saw him looking curiously into the rear bed. She moved quickly to join him and stared. "It looks moist."

"It's been cleaned. I mean cleaned! Look at this!" He gestured loosely to the ridges inside the truck's exposed bed. "Now take a look at the outside, around the sills, the front quarters."

Abigail backed up and leaned over in the direction he pointed, noticing a fair amount of dust and muddy residue on the exterior and inner wheel wells. "Go on," she commanded.

"This bed's been washed with something, soap maybe?" He ran his finger along the metal bottom and held it to his nose. "Doesn't smell like anything, but it's pretty clean."

"When?" she asked simply.

Steve considered the beads of water still in various places. "It could've been awhile ago. It's been humid. It's closed in here. Might take a couple days to evaporate. Maybe shorter. It's tough to tell."

"I assume you brought a cloth?"

He reached into his jacket pocket and removed another zip lock bag. "I brought two."

"Good. Do a sweep around the bed, and then do another around the driver's foot mat."

Steve nodded. "Understood."

"Make sure to use the whole cloth. I want to give a partial of each to Rick Parsons on our way back to Cheboygan."

Chapter 17

Heather felt a moment of vertigo as she peered down the steep incline of stone steps that led from the upper drive to the lower station. The way down was narrow and cut through a thick stand of hardwoods that filtered the sun and bathed the stairway in shifting patterns of yellow-green light and shade. She recovered and glanced back the way she'd come from the upper field and considered taking the long way around to avoid the sharp descent. A flicker of movement caught her attention as she saw Elise pass by below, walking quickly on the road near the bottom of the stairway.

"Elise!" she shouted to no avail, her voice lost among the white noise of the steady breeze coming up the hillside and through the surrounding woods. Heather thought of taking the upper road in the hope she'd intercept Peter's graduate student where the two roads came together a few hundred yards to the east, but she remembered the small parking lot below where it was likely Elise was headed.

She eyed the descent once again and placed a tentative foot on the narrow tread. The old steps once served as a main pathway to an upper clearing, where a enormous fire tower had at one time commanded the area, rising upward over a hundred feet above the tree line and giving a spectacular view of the surrounding lake from its lofty platform. Now the clearing was empty and had gone largely fallow, and few remained who knew why these stone steps cut so sharply into the hill.

Heather took each tread cautiously until she emptied into the sunshine of the dusty middle road and looked quickly to the right, seeing Elise retreating in the distance. "Elise!" she shouted again.

The student turned and watched as Heather walked quickly to intercept her. "Professor Wilkins?"

"I saw you pass by the bottom of the stairs back there," she said, pointing over her shoulder from where she'd shouted. "I want to talk to you. Do you have a minute?"

"Dr. Cummings wants me to assist him out on the branch," she said in an agitated voice. She removed her cell phone from her front pocket and looked at the face. "I was supposed to be there already but got delayed in a prep I've been doing on my own work."

"Did you say you're meeting him on the branch?"

Elise nodded. "Yes."

"The east branch?"

"Yes," she said insistently. "At his research site."

Heather decided to risk a direct approach. "Elise, were you aware Dr. Cummings saw Sondra Parker on the east branch the day she disappeared?"

The young woman's cheeks flushed slightly and her eyes widened, yet she remained silent.

"You realize the implication of this if it is true?" Heather hoped her tone suggested nothing threatening.

After several seconds, the young woman finally broke the silence, speaking tentatively, "Peter had nothing to do with what happened to Dr. Parker."

"I want to believe that, Elise," Heather insisted, "however, the fact remains Dr. Parker was drowned in Lake Kathleen, and it's my understanding he had some sort of interaction with her earlier that day on the river."

Heather was cautious not to reveal Rick's recent findings from the algal profile.

"Wait," Elise countered. "How do you know Peter had seen her that day?"

Heather eyed her carefully. "It's time for a measure of trust, ok? You were overheard speaking to him the other evening." She held up her hand to silence what looked like an attempt by Elise to deny anything. "It's none of my business why you were in the private company of your doctoral mentor, ok? I realize it was probably nothing, so there's no need to defend yourself. The fact is you were overhead talking to him, and Peter revealed he'd had an encounter with her on the river, is that correct?

The young woman's eyes softened slightly, and her shoulders seemed to relax. "Yes, that's correct."

"Do you realize how this looks?"

"Yes."

"Help me understand what took place. What did he tell you?"

#

"He was what?" Rick said incredulously.

"Scared," Heather answered.

"She told you that exactly? Peter was scared? Peter? Overconfident, overbearing, - "

"I get it," Heather interjected. "I think what she meant was something more like vulnerable."

Rick considered adding another unflattering adjective about their acerbic colleague but refrained when he saw her disapproval. "Go on," he said simply.

"According to Elise, Peter was standing in the shallows near the bank at his site, apparently dusting the Monkeyflower –"

"Dusting!" Rick interrupted. "You mean there's

pollen?"

"Evidently, yes. She said he'd collected trace amounts the day before and had returned in hope the stamens were producing more."

Rick's sat back, the realization coming to him. "So let me guess. Peter was in the river, his peaceful little kingdom. He was collecting what he knows is possibly a deal breaker for the project, and – "

"And Sondra happened to be in the same area doing a measurement," she added, noting a look of contrition on his face as she finished his thoughts. "Sorry, please continue."

"Thank you," he replied smugly. "She accidentally surprises him, and he freaks. I can only imagine knowing Peter. He's protective, and arrogant, and likely a little insecure. So there was an incident."

"Only words, according to Elise. Apparently Peter rather abruptly told her to, well, what I'd characterize as bugger off."

Rick chuckled at this. "And that's all?"

"That's what she said."

"So why not just be open about what happened?"

Heather gave him a confused look. "Do you mean Elise or Peter?"

"Peter. Why hide the fact he saw Sondra?"

"I can see two reasons. First, he didn't know David had overheard him telling Elise about the chance encounter. Second, my sense is he may have understandably worried he'd be implicated."

"Which is exactly what happened!" Rick then regretted his tone. "Sorry about that. It seems a little backward." He stared idly at the manila folder on the bench in front of him then turned his attention back to her. "What do you think?"

"About Peter? He's no killer. He's a pain and he's a

jerk, but I don't think he had anything to do with Sondra." Heather then glanced at the folder. "I've waited long enough, don't you think?"

"You're not supposed to be involved."

"And you said you thought Officer Bennett suspected me all along."

Rick tilted his head meaningfully at her. "Careful how you say that, all things considered."

"You know what I mean." She pointed to the folder. "I assume you finished working on what she dropped off yesterday."

Rick nodded. "Yeah. I did the work up."

"And?" her voice rose slightly.

"They brought me three cloth samples in the hope there'd be residues for analysis. I did a modified prep on each to wash them and ended up following the regular protocol for drying and mounting."

"And?" she said again more impatiently.

"The first sample came from Pritchard's waders. I got absolutely nothing from them. Not even the slightest trace."

"That can't be right!"

"It can if he washed them thoroughly and –"

"But even that should leave –"

"Will you let me finish?" he admonished her.

Heather winced slightly. "I apologize. Do go on, Professor."

"Abigail called with the results from their lab. They also ran the samples and found trace amounts of bleach on the cloth from the waders."

"Maybe he cleans his waders with bleach."

He looked at her strangely. "I don't think so. Picture Mike Pritchard getting home from fishing, taking his gear out of the back of his truck, and cleaning his waders with bleach. The second sample came from his truck bed. There were trace amounts of algae in the cloth." Rick finally opened the manila folder and extracted a piece of paper that contained a table. "Here's the diatom profile for the counts I did. You'll see it matches the profile for the east branch."

"Which isn't too surprising given he frequents the branch for fishing."

"Exactly," Rick said. "Same thing for the sample from the driver's floor mat."

"And there was nothing else from Officer Bennett's end?"

"Only that they tested for blood and the presence of the victim's DNA. The blood results came back negative in both truck samples. The DNA is still pending." Rick exhaled slowly and placed the sheet back into the folder. "If the DNA comes back with no finding, there's not much more that can be done."

"What about the circumstantial evidence?"

"Probably not enough. If Pritchard did it, and if he was careful about the body, there may be no way to get a positive – " Rick stopped suddenly, seeing a strange expression form on Heather's face.

"Heather?"

Her face registered something between shock and surprise, and she said breathlessly, "Of course! It should be right there."

"What are you talking about?"

"The samples! Do you still have some of the initial samples, prior to the prep work you did?"

Rick gestured to the far wall. "The tissues are still in the jars in the frig. I only cut away small portions of the cloths they gave me yesterday. The rest are in bags over there."

"I'll need a few hours," she said insistently.

"*You* will need a few –" and then it hit him. "You

think there might be - ?"

"I do," she said simply. "But I need you go find Peter as soon as possible."

He understood her meaning perfectly. "We don't have any here at the Station?"

She shook her head. "I already checked a couple weeks ago when I'd first heard about it. I wanted to see it for myself."

Rick looked at her admiringly. "Nicely done, teach."

"Go find him," Heather said anxiously.

#

"So what is so important you needed us to come over here right –" Abigail hesitated as she entered the lab with Steve and saw Heather standing next to the large window overlooking fishtail bay. She eyed Rick critically as they walked silently across the room and took their seats on the stools he'd pulled out for them to use.

"I believe you both know Professor Heather Wilkins of the Station," Rick said gesturing to her. Abigail continued to stare at him coolly before finally allowing the barest hint of smile to play out on her lips.

"Yes, you are the Palynologist here at the Station," Abigail said in a tone somewhere between a statement and an accusation. She turned to Steve and added succinctly, "She specializes in pollen," noting the bewildered expression on his face. She turned back to Heather. "And I think it's safe to assume you've been working with Professor Parsons here on the forensic investigation."

Heather decided upon an open approach. "Officer Bennett, I realize you'd given rather explicit instructions to Rick that he remain confidential in his clinical work. The truth is, I – " Heather stopped short, suddenly aware there was no easy way to explain the situation.

"The truth is," Rick chimed in, "I asked Heather to assist me with the forensic analysis, because I needed a colleague with whom I could discuss ideas, ensure proper technique and confirm any results I obtained."

Abigail glanced at Steve, who chuckled softly and simply shrugged his shoulders. "Well I suppose it can't be helped now. I was warned by a mutual friend that you might have certain complications with discretion."

"You mean Peg knows about our work?"

"Peg only knows that you are doing some lab analysis for me and nothing more. She was rather insightful about your, how should I put it, other interest."

Rick laughed softly, "Mea culpa."

Abigail turned to Heather. "And I suppose you are to lead this discussion, otherwise Rick would try to keep up the subterfuge."

"Oh, I like her," Heather said admiringly to Rick. "And yes," she said looking once again at Abigail, her face taking a more serious expression, "I want to show you my findings."

Heather retrieved a folder from the main table and stood holding it in front of the group. "I took the liberty of analyzing all the samples, though I did so with something else in mind. You see, Rick's acidic preparation protocol works perfectly fine for algal analysis, but it isn't appropriate for what I tend to study. Nitric acid is too harsh and usually destroys the exine coat, leaving nothing substantive to identify. This is ironic, for the outer walls are composed of organic compounds that are extremely resistant to chemicals, which is why we tend to find them well preserved in almost all conditions." Heather paused to see if there were any comments, and hearing none, she continued. "Once I removed the gross organics from the lung sample, I did the work up on it in a similar manner to the cloth swipes. Basically that involved removing any carbonate minerals and silicates and a subsequent prep to take out fine organics. I then concentrated each sample with a centrifuge and mounted small drops of the residue on a glass slide with a little glycerin."

She reached into the folder and extracted a piece of paper. "I did a count of roughly 200 grains for each sample and developed what we call an assemblage, which is another way of saying a pollen profile. You see, plants release pollen at various times, and so an assemblage reflects a local snapshot of the types and amounts of both wind and water borne pollen grains."

"And I assume you discovered a match between the victim and the other samples?" said Abigail.

"Yes," she said excitedly. "But whereas the diatom profile couldn't do more than confirm the victim was drowned in the east branch and that the suspect's vehicle-"

"Hold it! We're getting into a gray area here, Professor Wilkins," Abigail interrupted. "Since you have taken it upon yourself to do some forensic work for the benefit of the Cheboygan County Police Department, its important you refrain from drawing any conclusions about the evidence." Abigail noted the look of disbelief on Heather's face. "Please understand, should we need to use any evidence both you and Professor Parsons contributed in lets say a court proceeding, its fairly critical we keep a fine distinction between the investigator and the forensic specialist. Trust me, I mean no disrespect. Rather, I want to do this accordingly."

"I understand," replied Heather. "And so, let me say simply that I had a suspicion." She saw Abigail's eyes widen in alarm. "Not a suspicion like you are thinking. Rather, I had an idea that turned out to be, well, see for yourself." She handed her the piece of paper.

They studied it for nearly a minute until finally

Abigail looked up. "How is this possible?"

"As I said, the pollen assemblage is rather unique to a certain timeframe. It changes with a number of different factors – wind, weather, rain, and most certainly because of the unique timing of particular plants." Heather glanced to Rick, who nodded encouragingly. "The Station has a fairly impressive herbarium where we store samples of numerous botanical and aquatic specimens, including reference slides for algae and pollen. Two weeks ago, when Professor Cummings had raised his concerns about the Michigan Monkeyflower during Dr. Parker's presentation, I became curious to see if the Station even had any reference samples of its pollen. We didn't. Yesterday, however, when I was speaking with Dr. Cumming's graduate student, she told me he had begun to recover pollen from the recently blooming Monkeyflower in his research site on the east branch. Evidently, the flowers had started to produce pollen around the time Dr. Parker was tragically – " She stopped again, seeing a look of caution appear on Abigail's face.

"If I understand this correctly," said Abigail, gesturing loosely to the page she still held in her hand, "the victim's lung tissue had trace amounts of Monkeyflower pollen?"

"Yes," said Heather. "I was able to get a reference sample from Dr. Cummings yesterday, and I used this as the standard for identification of any grains in the subsequent samples."

"The counts were extremely low," Steve interjected.

"That's not surprising," said Heather. The majority of pollen in the assemblages along the branch would reasonably contain high levels of June pollinators, like certain late pines, summer grasses and various wildflowers which bloom during that time period. Of course, in the confines of the river basin, there's a preponderance of late pine and a few signatures from things like plantain and campion, both of which will grow in the sunny spots along the shore where the canopy is thin." Heather walked over and positioned herself behind them so she could point to the tables she'd created. "Still, there were measurable counts of Monkeyflower Pollen in the water sample from the east branch and in the victim's lung tissue. Furthermore," she added, pointing to the next table down, "I found counts of Monkeyflower pollen in the samples that came from the truck bed and the floor mat."

Steve sat back and whistled softly.

Abigail stared fixedly at the tables for several more seconds. Finally, she looked first to Rick and then shifted her gaze to Heather. "Any possibility of contamination?"

Heather shook her head slowly. "No. I've worked doing pollen preps proficiently long enough now to know how to keep things sterile between examinations."

Abigail handed the piece of paper back to her. "Nicely done, Professor Wilkins. Both of you, nicely done." She stood and motioned to Steve to do the same. "Looks like we need to return to Harbor Springs." She turned to Heather with an outstretched hand. "Thank you again. Make sure to do a complete write up on your protocol and findings. You too Rick. It's important to keep your data and samples secure, and of course let me stress again, you *must* keep all this to *yourselves*."

#

"You called for backup?"

Steve nodded and turned to her. "Dispatch is in contact with the Harbor Springs Police. We are to standby for an update." He then gestured over his shoulder. You were a little strict on her back there."

Abigail stayed silent as she turned the car onto Riggsville Road out of the Station and sped west toward the direction of Harbor Springs. "I'm planning ahead, that's all."

"Let me guess, the attorneys."

"His defense will do everything to get the case thrown out, including calling into question the methods and integrity of the expert testimony. Those two have done well, but the defense will undoubtedly try to cast doubt on their experience."

Steve regarded her earnestly. "Do you think the Monkeyflower evidence is enough?"

"Yes. However, ultimately it will depend on how the jury sees it."

"How do you think it happened?"

"Likely he accidentally stumbled upon her in the branch. Who knows? Could be he intentionally sought her out. Hit her with a blunt object. Andrew said it was a rock."

Steve nodded.

"She lost consciousness, and he drowned her in a deep pool. She took the river water into her lungs, with the pollen and algae from upstream, among other things. Its unbelievable, really."

"And then he put her body in the truck."

"Carefully. My guess is he wrapped her head to keep the blood from contaminating everything. He must have dumped her in Kathleen later that night."

The hollow voice of dispatch interrupted. "Be advised of backup arriving to State Road in fifteen minutes."

Abigail reached over and pushed the mike button. "Roger backup. Have all assistance hold at the intersection of State and Stutzmanville until we arrive in twenty. Bennett out."

Epilogue

Heather studied a pair of chickadees perched on a tube feeder in the small grassy area beside the restaurant then allowed her gaze to shift to the distant view of Lake Kathleen several hundred yards downhill and partially obscured by the undulating landscape. Its surface glistened deep blue in the evening sun, creating a picturesque image for the diners to enjoy.

"I wonder what will happen," she said softly, turning her eyes toward him.

"I think the die was already cast."

"You still don't believe Peter's finding will be enough to halt the project?"

Rick shook his head slowly. "Unfortunately, no. The project was going to go through despite their knowing about the viable patch at the bottom of the dam." He pointed out the window toward the descending road that vanished around a curve. "If they were willing to take a gamble on the restoration not changing the hydrology significantly for a plant they already knew about, I seriously doubt another will make much difference. Peter's new discovery probably won't be affected that much, at least as far as hydrology."

Heather cast her eyes about the restaurant, now crowded with summer people all come to enjoy their yearly anticipation. "What about this place?"

"It'll go on just fine." He glanced out the window

to the distant water. "That'll be gone, and it's going to look a little scoured down there for awhile." He turned back to her. "Still, a couple years and the green will come back in. Eventually, it'll go through its own natural succession."

"What about the name?"

"The plan is to remove most of the dam structure and lower the lake slowly over the course of several weeks. I read they're planning to leave a portion of the dam as a foundation for a new bridge to be built across the restored river."

"No more Lake Site Inn it would seem."

Rick shrugged. "Who knows, perhaps Miles should change the name to Dam Site Inn to reflect the restoration."

"I saw you speaking with him quietly before we were seated. Was he asking about the arrest?"

"And about the project status. I think he's just relieved to have the matter settled."

"Do you mean the murder?"

"Yeah. He's relieved not to be a suspect, that's clear enough."

Heather reached for her wine glass and took a long drink. Out of the corner of her eye, she saw the well-dressed form of Miles Kirnan escorting an elderly couple to a waiting table near a corner window. "I guess you're right," she said softly, setting her glass back on the white tablecloth and meeting Rick's eyes once more. "Things will likely turn out ok."

"Which reminds me," Rick said with a change of tone as he lifted his glass. "A toast."

She returned the gesture, her face a mixture of curiosity and hope.

"Here's to us working things out for the best."

Heather hesitated as she brought the glass to her lips. "You mean the case?"

He laughed then, warmly, and reached across the table to take her hand. "No. I had something else in mind."

She paused for a moment, before allowing her lips to form a mischievous smile. "The Bug Camp won't be the same, you know."

He laughed again. "I guess things have a way of changing after all."

"For the better," she added.

Rick looked out the window toward Lake Kathleen and pictured the river restored, its water flowing unbroken from Douglas Lake through the countryside below. He thought of the cottages along the lake's shoreline, set back from the warm summer water within the deep greens of the northern woods. He pictured the trails in Grapevine Point, and the tin can shacks of the Bug Camp, of the Big Shoal and Fishtail, and the breaking waves that spilled against the eastern sands, where wild mint grows unspoiled from one year to the next.

"Rick?"

He turned his eyes to her once again. "Mostly, it's still the same, and that's a very good thing."

She smiled then and squeezed his hand. "Then, let's head back home."

Author's Notes:

During the period when I was completing the final editing of this story, the project to remove the Woodland Road dam had begun, and Lake Kathleen was being slowly drained over the course of several weeks.

Though this is a work of fiction, my descriptions of the pros/cons of the restoration of the Maple River closely align with the truth. There is a temperature differential between the upper branches and the lower stem, which have a bearing on the quality of fishing along what was an interrupted riparian corridor from Lake Kathleen. There was (and still is) a notable concern of the potential negative effect of predatory fish migrating further up into the east and west branches once the dam had been removed.

The threatened status of the Michigan Monkeyflower is accurately represented. There are only a handful of these plants known to exist, and the current patch beneath the former dam along Woodland Road is one of the few to produce viable pollen. Now that the dam has been removed, it is arguable the resultant hydrology will have little to no impact on this sensitive flowering plant. I wouldn't be surprised to learn that this location becomes extinct.

Of course, I have taken a few liberties for the purposes of enhancing the story. For example, though there is trout fishing along the Maple River, the east branch is simply too narrow and subject to dry periods where the water level gets too low to support much in the way of good sport fishing. The west branch is actually preferable and colder on account of more numerous springs.

The University of Michigan Biological Station (The "Bug Camp") is a wonderful institution on the south shore of Fishtail Bay on Douglas Lake. Growing up as a child and young adult during the formative summers of my life, I, much like the main character, looked upon the researchers there with a measure of curiosity. I used to wonder how anyone could be so fascinated with an interest in insects and wildflowers, trees and microbes. I am relieved that I have matured since those summers of my youth and now I regard their passions as most wondrous and worthy of admiration.

Douglas Lake is the place where my thoughts often go, and where one day my spirit will come to rest among the tall pines and the shifting winds that blow across the warm water.

Made in the USA
Coppell, TX
30 October 2019